This is, as ever, dedicated gratefully to my mom,

the greatest influence on my life,

and to The Sophie,

the greatest influence on my future.

Best Served Cold

By John G. Walker

Acknowledgements

There are an incredible amount of awesome and wonderful people who got me this far. This list is by no means comprehensive or complete. It's just I am so humbled and amazed at how wonderful and fortunate I am to have these people in my life.

My mom. Tied for my biggest cheerleader, she's the one who always said she had no idea what I was talking about, but it sounded pretty cool. The times when you told me that I could do whatever I wanted if I worked hard enough, I took them to heart. Look, Ma! I'm an author! I always want to make you proud, Mom. I hope I have.

My niece. The Sophie is my other cheerleader. Her sense of wonder and imagination is what helps fuel mine, and for that, I am ever in her debt. My message to you, my young apprentice, is this: The magic is real. Never stop believing in it. Don't let anyone tell you otherwise.

My sister and brother-in-law. They deal with my insanity and my asking of questions that probably have me on several no-fly lists. Thank you for not having me committed when I asked about, well, pretty much anything.

My grandmother. There's so much to say about this lady, but suffice it to say, she always kept me going, whether I liked it or not. I love you, Chief.

My editor. Erika Pryor is essentially the direct inspiration for Rika Elder. She's also just an outstanding editor, and this series would never have gotten off the ground without her. Thank you, Pryor.

Dave Robison. My mentor. My friend. The man to blame and thank for my continuing the journey through my mind and soul to bring out the hunks of dirty yellow thought so they could be transmuted into gleaming literary gold. Thank you. For everything.

The folks at the Dead Robots Society podcast. Terry Mixon, Justin Macumber, Paul Cooley, and Scott Roche. You are four impossibly talented authors, and your books challenged me to be a better writer. I learned from you four, and I hope I learned those lessons well. Thank you for the lessons and the entertainment.

Starla Huchton. Your talent in making gorgeous covers to wrap around my stories is matched by your incredible ability to weave tales of such complexity and talent, I can't help but be awed. My thanks to you for helping me look like I know what I'm doing.

The Round Table Novel Writing Month group. Every single one of you have my unending thanks for listening to my ideas, of being supportive, and knowing how to be critical in a way that didn't stifle me, but free me.

I have to single out Gus and Erin, the hosts of the Melting Potcast. My friends, my fans, and the first podcast to do a really in-depth interview. You have no idea how amazing that was, and I treasure our friendship.

For anyone I missed, I'm sorry, but know that you are awesome, and thank you for everything.

Now, it's time to dive in to this, the seventh volume of The Statford Chronicles. Enjoy, everyone, and see you on the other side.

-jgw

Chapter One

Sometimes, it just doesn't pay to get out of bed.

My eyes shot open, the sounds of cars going by outside waking me with the horns blaring and engines running. My feet hit the floor of my bedroom, which was more a closet in my office than anything else. I spent a lot of time at my office since my return, mainly because I had nowhere else to go. For two weeks, I had done little except sleep, eat, and catch up on current events, and for the latter, things had gotten stranger than usual. I don't mean "supermodel named her child after a body part and kitchen appliance" weird, but "epic realignment of beliefs and entities inhabiting our realm of existence" weird.

Although just to be fair, Appendix Toaster Oven is a stupid name for a kid.

I felt pain spear my heart again at the thought of children. Though it had been years for everyone else, it seemed only a scant three weeks for me since I had watched my wife Susana get brutally sacrificed in a ritual designed to end the world. A cult of lunatics kidnapped the both of us after we found their warehouse lair, then killed her in front of me, all in an insane attempt to bring about a cataclysmic shift in the universe.

The Reader's Digest version of the results: It worked.

The more expanded version of the results: the gods were pulled down from their respective realms to this one, the "real" world. It was a crazy plan, an insane idea. That's the problem with some insane ideas: they sometimes manage to happen, and the rest of the world just has to deal with the consequences. Not only that, but we have to keep dealing with it. The only ones who never have to deal with it again are the dead, and in those days, the time following the Fall, even the dead were restless.

I ran the fingers of my left hand through the slow-growing dark hair that would eventually cover the scar on the side of my head. I leaned over and pulled my Colt Python out from under my pillow with my right hand. It was a chrome monster with a six-inch barrel, and I could see my brown eyes reflected in the metal. They were still rimmed with red, whether from broken sleep or broken dreams. I had lost a lot in the prior two years. My wife, my family, my identity as Thomas Statford, and only the latter two were back in my possession. Susana was lost to me.

With a practiced motion, I opened the cylinder and checked the loads. Six pristine firing pins stared back at me, winking in the sunlight streaming through the window. I closed the cylinder and put it back down on the bed, under the pillow and out of sight, but not out of mind.

"Not today," I whispered, my breathing slow but my heart jackhammering. Every morning since my return, I would take the gun out, check the bullets, and put the gun back. It had become almost a ritual; I didn't want to break it.

Besides, there was someone else much more worthy of a .357 jacketed hollow-point, and I would find them, or die trying.

"Thomas? Are you awake?" Most people would have freaked out at the head and shoulders sticking itself through the closed door. I was not only used to it, but expected it. The flowing blonde hair and crystal-blue eyes were things I had missed for two years without knowing I was missing them. Those eyes had seen more than six thousand years of history, and the spirit was still learning about the world. Larrisimus, or Larry, as I called him, had never lied to me, at least not on purpose.

"Yeah, I am now," I muttered, sitting up straight and stretching. The crackle of my spine was audible, and Larry winced as he pulled himself completely into my room. "He still there?"

"Of course," Larry said, "as are others."

I grunted as I pulled on a pair of jeans. There was a pair of black sweatpants neatly folded on a dresser near me, but I avoided them with a shudder. Too many memories were attached to sweatshirts and sweatpants. "The others," I said. "Are they here on Conclave business, or should I finish dressing?"

The Conclave. Not as powerful as it was before, but still a force to be reckoned with. See, when this universe, or multiverse, depending on what you believe, was young, there were gods. Yes, multiple pantheons of gods exist, all at the same time, and for the first few billion years, they got along as well as the Donner party would get along with the Mansons. Worlds and galaxies died and were recreated at their whim, trillions of lives ended and restarted just for the sheer joy of creation and destruction. The width and breadth of Creation was their playground, and the gods used and abused it as they saw fit.

Of course, that couldn't last, so they decided it would be a good idea to stop being fools before they brought all of existence to a crushing, crashing halt. Thus was born the Conclave, which became, for lack of a better term, the United Nations of the pantheons. It was pretty simple on the surface: each pantheon would respect the boundaries of the others, and no one, especially us mere mortals, would get hurt. However, there were always going to be problems between one faction or another. Gods were about as stable as your average table with three and a half legs during an earthquake.

Enter the Keeper, or at least the mantle of the Keeper. The gods decided it would be a good idea to have a mortal representative, someone in between them and mortals, who could act as an emissary, a mediator, and when necessary, a protector. Until about two and a half years before, I had done that with only a few complaints. Of course, my complaints included several broken bones, numerous scars over various parts of my body, likely irreparable psychic damage from a demon mucking about in my head, and a plethora of other horrid and horrible things that I seemed to have started getting used to shoving in the back of my mind to deal with later.

That was all before the Fall. The media tried their damnedest to come up with something snazzier: The Cataclysm, the Ruination, the Apocalypse. All very adorably pants-wetting- fear inducing, and all quickly forgotten in the days and weeks following the event. Some wit had thought to try and call it the Skyfall, but got shut down pretty quickly by the folks who own the trademark. After that, it was simply called the Fall.

People tried wrapping their brains around it, the idea that the gods could be pulled down to Earth. It wasn't exactly something anyone expected; after all, what happens when every religious text is wrong in the word but not the spirit? What happens when you can actually run into not only the deity you worship in Sunday School on the street, but the ones worshipped thousands of years ago, and actually converse with them? That was bad for most, and there had been a great many people who couldn't handle it and opted for the other way out. That wasn't including the thousands who lost their lives in the flare-up of holy wars and blasting enemies to bits in the name of some deity or another. Granted, mortals usually didn't need any excuse to do stupid things like that, but thankfully, the idiocy ended quickly, in no small part thanks to some strong-arming by the gods themselves and some people I knew very well.

The t-shirt was a simple navy blue, a bit on the big side, which worked for me as I pulled it over my head. I wasn't a big fan of the color anymore, but I couldn't be choosy. I hadn't worn much besides jeans and t-shirts for most of my life, and after dropping back into my life without any warning, I had very little clothing that actually fit anymore. My time in the faux-mental institution had made me lose weight, nearly to the point of emaciation. Two years before, I weighed in the neighborhood of two hundred pounds. When I stepped on a scale two weeks prior, I was barely a buck-fifty. Granted, it was nearly pure muscle, but I wasn't used to my sharp, angular features when I looked down at my body and in the mirror. I looked like a cadaver back from the dead, and perhaps in a way I was.

"I'll be out in a minute, Larry," I said, pulling a belt tight around my waist. It wasn't for style; my pants were so loose on me the legs felt like sails flapping in the breeze. "Just need to take care of something first."

"Of course, Thomas." Larry had been especially conscientious of my needs since my return, keeping his usual snark and sarcasm to so much a minimum I almost felt he was mocking me with his sincerity. He was much more solemn than the airy and verbose spirit who accompanied me on cases and adventures over a span of a decade. I wondered what happened to him while I was out of circulation, and made a mental note to ask when time and opportunity permitted.

I did my first set of thirty pushups in less than a minute, keeping a steady rhythm going down and coming up. After that, I rolled onto my back and tucked my feet, still bare, under the twin bedframe. Fifty crunches in under a minute, and I was barely breathing heavily. Though the space was tight, I rolled onto my stomach and stood, beginning a set of thirty squats. On the tenth squat, I grabbed a nearby weight off the small dresser.

My room could charitably be called a cell, being only eight feet by twelve feet, but it was big enough for one person to sleep and live. The bed dominated most of one side, while a small shower, barely big enough for me before I left, took up six square feet at the southwestern corner of the room. An old dresser, beaten down by age and use, took up a bit more space, leaving me just enough to do my morning workout. I had started it in the asylum, and continued it with even more ferocity. The ten-mile run I would do after I had disposed of my guests, or tried to, at least.

After five sets of each exercise, I was finally starting to breathe heavily and sweat from exertion. The pace I set was grueling as I doubled the number of repetitions. My lungs began to burn from the air running in and out of my lungs, the breath laced with moisture. The muscles in my arms screamed in agony, and I ignored them, focusing on the pain, harnessing it, knowing it was going to be used elsewhere and elsewhen. I took that hurt, that anguish, and pushed it into a small box in the back of my brain, where it could grow and feed on itself and become a white-hot coal of wrath. I tortured myself because I would be paying back the motherfucker who took my wife every bit of the pain and then some.

And when I was through, I would begin all over again.

The entire regimen lasted thirty minutes, and when I rolled onto my back to catch my breath, I began to perform what was called chi-breathing. Inhale the good chi, exhale the bad. Over and over I performed the simple routine, not letting the exhale take away of the fire in my mind. I took great care to keep that anger and hatred in my mind, and not let it seep anywhere else. I wanted cold and calculating anger and vengeance, so frigid it burned the flesh away to the bone, so sharp it flayed the muscles to strips of meat. I didn't know who was behind it all, nor did I know what I would face to get to the one who gave the order, and I really did not care. I wanted blood, and I would have it, or die trying.

My five minutes of breathing completed, I stripped off the t-shirt and put on another one bearing the visage of Leonard Nimoy staring severely out at the world. Arrayed around his face were the words "I grok Spock." I envied his fictional ability to push away everything emotional and look at everything in austere logic. I wished I could just let it all go.

And if my aunt had balls she'd be my uncle, I snarled to myself, trying to pull myself out of the funk that was starting around me. I pushed the feelings aside, putting on a brave face, and went out to meet my guests and, hopefully, get rid of them as quickly as possible. There was work to do, and I needed all the time I could get to prepare.

The smile was as genuine as a whore's orgasm, and lasted about as long, but it served its purpose of camouflage as I surveyed my office. Outside the windows I could see the early January sky, clear, blue, and blamelessly innocent of clouds. The natural light was much better than artificial, and I sucked up the little bit extra cost to have the insulated windows rather than keep them covered by curtains. My desk was covered in even in spacing but not in height piles of paper, something I wasn't expecting upon my return. The mellow wood glowed from a few new layers of varnish that was added in my absence, and it did the furniture an immense amount of good, making it look almost new even though it was older than I was. There were a few rugs tossed hither and yon, with one in front of the low couch and another placed before a simple brown leather chair. The filing cabinets with tales of my cases were in their place, as was the refrigerator with drinks and snacks and other things for consumption. Every morning, I drank deeply of my office, Spartan though it was. The office was a place of normalcy, even with a storm of strangeness, of the weirdness, going on all around it. It was a haven against all the horrors and oddities I faced and, gods help me, would face again.

For the moment, it was time to get to work.

"Tom." Mister Renton was seated in the leather chair, his back to me. I recognized the broad shoulders, dark hair, and immaculately-tailored suit immediately. The only time I had seen him out of the Giorgio Armani suit was when he caught a piece of shrapnel in his lung, a parting gift of one of the doomsday cult. He seemed no worse for wear as he smoothly glided to his feet, towering over me by a few inches. Renton's ruddy complexion was a bit lighter than when I left before, likely from him staying in more northern climates. What I knew about the man for certain could be written on an index card with room to spare. However, he was loyal to my mom, which made him aces in my book. I glanced at the bulge beneath his left armpit and caught sight of his weapon, likely the .40 Smith and Wesson he preferred, as his coat opened slightly. My eyes, trained by my mother, missed nothing as he flicked a sky-blue glance at the other living occupant.

Rika Elder made her presence known with her usual subtlety. "Bout time you woke up, princess. We've been waiting for hours." The Memphis twang was almost completely hidden, and only came out when she was truly on the warpath. I had known Rika for years, when she had started as a beat cop and I had just gotten my start in the weirdness. We were close in those days, and I owed the lady thanks for introducing me to her partner, Susana. From such humble beginnings are legends born. Rika was actually seated at my desk, going over a few pages of hard copy, looking for something that meant something to her. As I had just walked in, I was clueless about her search. The sunlight gave her mocha skin a glow, and a glint of light in her dark hair spoke of a golden headband of some kind. She was wearing a thick leather coat, which told me just what she thought of my keeping the heat off at night.

"You have not," I said, smiling slightly to take some sting off my words. "Maybe an hour, but sure as hell not more than one."

Renton walked over to me hesitantly. He seemed unsure what to say, shifting from one foot to another. I felt sorry for the guy; if I could have prompted him to say what was on my mind, I would have. However, I had learned patience, and made it a habit to practice it as often as possible. Renton's eyes cut over to Rika again, and I saw the slight nod of her head. With her permission, he took the plunge.

"I'm sorry I failed you, Tom," he began, his words full of pain. "I wasn't there to help you and Susana. I should have been there. I failed you and," he looked at his hands in anguish, "I failed your mother. Since you didn't say anything before, I felt I should be the one to speak of it. I will tender my resignation to your mother today." He looked me in the eye, the barest hint of tears in his own. It was the closest I had ever seen him come to actual emotion, and it touched me more than his words. So maybe my first reaction to his apology wasn't the best.

I laughed.

It wasn't a little chuckle, either. It was that long, deep, gut-busting laughter that begins at the heels and rolls up the entire body and out the mouth. I shuddered from mirth and actually needed to brace myself on both Renton and my desk to remain standing. Whenever I felt the laughter begin to taper off into burbles of giggles, I would see Renton's confused face and then I'd be off to the races again.

After a few minutes, I finally got myself under some semblance of control and shook my head. "You stone-brained son of a bitch, if you resign, I will personally have your ass kicked," I pointed at Rika, "by her." I clapped him on the shoulder and continued. "That is, of course, after my mom beats the living hell out of you for thinking you failed. You didn't." I made my way over to the fridge and grabbed a cold bottle of water out of it. Two years before it would have been a Diet Dew. My, how times changed. "You performed admirably, and did the best you could. We were all wrong."

"What happened—" Renton began before I interrupted him.

"Was unforeseen." Gods, I sounded calmer than I really was. In the back of my head, the ball of fire roared. "I don't hold you responsible at all for what happened. If anything, it was my fault, and I take responsibility for it. It's okay, Renton. I promise."

I could see her pursed lips with my peripheral vision and I heard a low mumble of "Told you" from Rika as she rolled her eyes. Renton bowed his head and nodded, then reached into his pocket and pulled out his wallet. A piece of green paper with Benjamin Franklin fluttered down in front of Rika, disappearing before it touched the blotter. I walked past Renton to the window, Rika on my left, and I let my eyes take in the world outside.

A world that was changed impossibly, if what Larry told me was even remotely accurate.

"So what leads do we have?" I put my hands in my pockets past the wrists, if only to keep the shakes from starting.

My words rang in the room, bouncing off the glass and hard wood. When I repeated myself, I turned around. Renton looked at me curiously, while Rika began putting the pieces of paper in a manila envelope. The silence became a bit much, so I opened my mouth to ask a third time. Rika pushed back from my desk and speared me with a look.

"There are no leads, Tom." Her words flummoxed me, but she continued. "There's nothing out there, and believe me, we looked."

"Bullshit!" The word was out of my mouth before I could draw it back. Taking a deep breath, I continued calmly. "Sorry. You're telling me there's nothing out there? Nothing at all about a well-connected and clued-in bunch of nuts doing human sacrifice?"

Renton sighed. "We went over the area with a fine-tooth comb repeatedly, Tom. If there was anything there, we'd have found it."

"We did," Rika confirmed. "I had every single square inch of that place covered by a microscope. There was nothing there." She paled as much as she could, then amended her words. "I mean, other than, you know…"

"The bodies of a dozen crazies and Susana," I finished. "All of them with their hearts cut out." My hands curled into fists, muscles thrumming with tension. With a conscious effort, I opened my fists and put my palms on the frigid glass. "I know what you found, Rika. I was there."

"Not when we got there. It was horrible." Rika shuddered as she stood up. "Blood and bodies everywhere, with chests cut open and---" She paused and walked to Renton, who put a comforting hand on her shoulder. "Tommy, it was like Hell opened up."

"You missed something." I was adamant, and I didn't know why. Something in my head wanted me to go there, even though I thought my soul would break from being in that abattoir again. I glanced at Larry. "We're going." I walked to the office door. "Come on, Larry."

"Thomas," the spirit said, "I think these two are correct. They did not miss anything."

"*E tu*, Larry?" I laughed with a mirth hollow in my ears. "Something is there, and you all missed it."

Renton stepped forward, arms crossed over his chest. "Tom, I assure you, we have been over that place a dozen times in two years. Your mother even leased the place in perpetuity in case you returned there. It's been searched repeatedly over the last two years in hopes of finding where you went. If there were something there, we would have found it long ago."

I shrugged my shoulders and made my way to my desk. Picking up the desk phone with my right hand, I opened up a drawer with my left. I pulled out several large bills, part of a rainy day fund that I kept in case of emergencies.

"Who are you calling?" Rika snapped at me.

"A cab. If I can't get you all to give me a ride, I'll just have to call one."

A tinny voice on the phone gave the name of a cab company in a bored tone. It was cut off abruptly by Renton putting his finger on the hook. "You know we can't let you go alone."

"I won't be alone," I retorted. "Larry will be there."

"We'll take you, and show you we didn't miss anything." Renton got a coat for me. "Here, it looks nice out there, but it's still a bit frosty."

I pulled the warm pea coat on, glad it was in a non-blue color. "Where'd you get this?"

"Your mom dropped it off last night," Rika smiled. "She knew you wouldn't stay in this place any more than you needed to get ready."

Nodding my head, I put most of the money back in the drawer, keeping a few bills to shove in my pocket. In the right pocket, I felt something hard and metal. I didn't let myself react, but left the money deep in the pocket. "Okay, then, let's go."

"Thomas," Larry said, his voice hesitant. "We do not need to go. What do you hope to find there?"

Looking over at Renton and Rika, I gave a half-smile. To Larry, I said, "The starting line." I opened the door to the outside, a bracing breeze stinging my face. "The beginning of the end."

"The end of what, Thomas?"

Steel entered my voice as I looked over my shoulder. "The end of the motherfucker who killed her."

Chapter Two

One thing I never figured, Renton being was a lover of the classics.

This was a guy who spent most of his life working with some of the most high-tech gadgets the world had to offer. My mom was notorious for not going with the lowest bidder, at least from what I could tell from the amount of equipment that was on hand at any given time. Results mattered to her, and also to Renton. When we finally left my office, I thought Renton was driving the cherry red Jaguar. Sleek and sexy, it was a hell of a car, crouched in its parking spot like its namesake. There was a raw power to it that purred in barely restrained pleasure. The sheen on it showed that someone loved that Jaguar, which made me think of the Beauty, my black Chevy Tracker, lost to explosives planted by madmen years ago.

Before the train of thought could go any further, I hit the brakes on it. The loss of one led to the loss of another, and I wasn't prepared to go into that pain. Not yet, anyway.

So it was with some surprise that Renton bypassed the Jag with a sneer and opened the door to a 1970 Chevrolet Chevelle SS. I wasn't much of a car guy, but I knew what I liked, and I've always had a soft spot for a Chevy. This darling was a pure classic, with a pearlescent black paint job covering the chassis, and, from the starting of the engine, a real 454-cubic-inch V8 under the hood that sounded like the roaring of a thousand lions. It was so beautiful, it nearly brought a tear to my eye. As I got into the backseat so Rika could join Renton in the front, I luxuriated in the feel of leather against my hands and the softness contained underneath it. I could tell it was real leather, the kind that would make a vegan retch and a member of PETA scream bloody murder. This wasn't just a car; it was a labor of love.

I buckled up as Rika took her seat in front. "Nice wheels, Renton," I called out.

A ghost of a smile crossed his face; I could see him in the rearview mirror. With his characteristic modesty, he said, "It gets me around." He put it into drive and started driving, first down King Street, then onto Mercury Boulevard, the main drag that went straight through Hampton.

Rika snorted. "'It gets me around,'" she mocked his deep voice, the words like a bullfrog. "He restored this thing himself over a year ago and you would think it was a gift brought down from the heavens being wrought by angels like the ark of the covenant." There was another snort, this time of laughter. "This monkey treats his car better than he does anything else."

As the two bantered back and forth, I tuned their voices out. There was love there, which was important, of course, but there was also that mutual respect, which meant even more. That was the kind of thing epic romances were built on, and even in my extremity of emotion, I could see that those two kids would be either the best of friends and lovers, or the kind of enemies that would make Bond villains shake in fear. I didn't need to pay much attention to the two of them; I knew they were made for each other, no matter how much hell one gave the other. It brought a wisp of a smile to my face, tired as it was.

Even considering my dealings with the divine and the demonic over the years, I only saw them perform minor stuff, such as immolation of a human being or vanishing in a flash of light. Soon after becoming the Keeper, I asked Hermes, the messenger of the Greek gods and a deity in his own right, why his fellows weren't flashier with their power. After all, I reasoned, you're gods. What's the point of all that power if you don't use it?

Hermes laughed and told me the other gods enjoyed using the tools of the times when dealing with humanity. What was the difference between a bolt of lightning and a bullet to the heart? Nothing mattered but the results, as far as the gods were concerned. Sometimes a bit of flexing the old deity muscle was needed, he allowed, but most of the time, it was the followers who did the will of the gods, rather than the gods themselves. No need to be flashy about it. A low profile meant fewer dust-ups between the pantheons. No one liked a show-off.

So it was quite a shock for me to see the gods everywhere. Literally everywhere.

As Renton got his roadbeast roaring up to the speed limit on the interstate, I gawked in amazement at the various gold, silver, platinum, copper and stone roofs for the multitude of temples, along with their attendant flashing signs denoting them as places of worship for Hera, or Set, or Amaterasu, or a double-dozen others. Each sign gave the promise of food, drink (especially at the temples of Bacchus), sex, or some mixture of the three. There were still the "normal" places, like the Padre Martin's church off Interstate 64, the mosque of Imam Amir abd al-Mohammed, and Rabbi Jordan Harel's temple, but they were surrounded by buildings of so many different supreme beings, it was a wonder none of them had stepped on each other's toes, at least property-wise.

If the signs had made me gape, then I didn't want to know what I looked like as I watched several winged creatures soar across the sky. Some of them were miles in the air, my naturally sharp vision picking them out against the clouds and the blue. Others were close to the ground, and I mean close. A few were a scant hundred feet off the ground, their serpentine scaled tails and bodies held aloft by a pair of relatively thin outstretched membranes. Smoke and steam trailed from their nostrils, razor-sharp talons winking in the late morning sun.

Soaring between these flying lizards were lithe forms wearing cassocks or tunics, pure white feathers flapping lazily. Several had long swords at their belts, while some had huge maces and flails taking the place of a blade. They were graceful, all of them, and painfully beautiful, with flawless skin, muscled limbs and glowing features, though I think the last was due to the halos hanging over their heads. There had been a run-in or three with their general a few years ago, which ended surprisingly well for me, as I was still alive to talk about it, thanks to a priest who wasn't always a priest. Michael was known for his fury; I was a witness to it at one time. Thankfully, the only thing the ones who flew above us wanted to do was get from one place to another.

I knew I was gawking like a tourist, and I couldn't give a damn less. At one time, this world was as normal as it could get. Sure, there were the occasional massacres at schools, and suicide bombers, and horrible natural disasters that ended the lives of thousands, but those were things of a mundane sort. We could point to the idiot who pulled the trigger on a bunch of kids and say it was that dumb bastard's fault. The buck stopped on this world, and we could, maybe not understand it, but at least comprehend it.

The thing is, once you add the reasons why most of those nutballs did what they did, namely the gods, walking around and talking and having a latté, that adds a whole new level of problems, and a whole lot of perspective. It also allowed the gods to voice their displeasure, which they did. From what I read on the news archives, they voiced it loud and often. The gods rarely did things in half-measures, and affronts to their sovereignty ranked at the top of the list of ways to piss them off.

According to some of the priests of Ares, there were some swaths of land the size of Delaware that might one day stop burning. Maybe.

"How bad is it out there?" I pointed to the sky.

Rika answered me. "It's calmed down a hell of a lot. No one really knew how to handle it when all the things and people of myth and legend showed up with no clue what was going on and ready to fight." She turned to look at me over the seat. "It's hard to get a good number, but it's thought over three million people died that first day." My look of horror must have shown. "Mostly to accidents and heart failure. Nothing the gods themselves did, but just their arrival. It got worse after they announced themselves. That's when the suicides started."

"Suicides?"

"I guess when you have direct proof that what you've been told your entire life is a lie, it can fuck you up in the head." Rika turned to face the front. "Most of it made Jonestown look like bible camp, and in a way it was. It was really terrible, Tommy. I had to visit a couple of places around here that decided to take the quick way out." Her voice went to stone. "There were baby bottles all over the place with arsenic and red kool-aid."

I rubbed my hand over my face, trying to take in all the information I could and still maintain a level of sanity and detachment. Whether I liked it or not, those deaths were on my head, the blood on my hands. Whatever it was I did two years before, what started with Susana, led to millions of deaths. "I take it there's more?"

Renton took up the thread of the story, taking an exit to Newport News I wasn't familiar with. "Of course. When the gods came down, they got worshippers. It became equal opportunity for every single stupid religion to get its name in the papers and their faces on television. Some of the cults were the 'fun' kind."

"Like Dionysus," I said, naming a god of drink and revelry.

"Or Aphrodite. Their meetings can be somewhat," he paused, "energetic. Unfortunately, there were hundreds of others who decided to get into the game, and their followers were quite a bit less enjoyable."

"Ares, I take it?"

"That would be one of them," Renton nodded. "There's one called Apep who's a real nasty bastard."

I sighed. Serpent god for folks who call all snakes evil, the Egyptians. So much of an asshole that ancient Egyptians actively worshipped against him. Like the world needed something like that unleashed on it with all the other fun and wonderful destructive forces unleashed upon it. "So it was all of them that got brought down. Lovely."

"It's worse than that, but we'll have to talk about that later," Renton said. "We're here."

Never before had two such innocuous words filled me with such dread. To my surprise, we were near the Newport News airport, a place of bustling activity and people flying to and from the area in droves. Renton was parked near a hanger so far outside the main buildings of the airport it could almost be called its own private terminal. I looked around for some frame of reference, some buried memory from the years ago and the Big Empty in my head that would ring a bell, but there was nothing. This building, set in the middle of a field that was empty save a small runway, was anonymous to me.

I got out of the Chevy with great hesitation, after Rika exited. The hanger's foundation was overgrown with weeds, both living and dead. Kudzu was entwined in the walls, snaking in and out of whatever holes it could find in its journey to the roof. Nature was winning against the structures of humanity as the greenery sprouted in various places across the metal I could see. The air had warmed up to where I could no longer see my breath, which made me consider the kudzu.

"Bit cold for that crap, isn't it?" I nodded to the plants.

Renton smiled thinly. "Call it a gift from one of the nature goddesses who landed here. The overgrowth used to be a nightmare. Even now, the plants grow all year around the airport. Their hardiness drives the developers crazy."

When I raised an eyebrow in question, Rika laughed. "They were trying to tear the field up and put in some condos or some high rise monstrosity." She reached down and picked one of the dandelions at her feet. The moment she did so, another small yellow flower shot up from the earth. "Nature won; and kept winning." Rika pointed off to the east. "You can barely see the tops of the bulldozers that were pulled under. That shit was hilarious."

I shook my head at the idea of the earth opening up and swallowing tons of metal and machine, and I didn't ask which nature goddess was the culprit. Knowing would change nothing, and I had more important things on my plate. I pulled the still-chilled air into my lungs and held it, letting my senses take in every single bit of data they could so I could get an idea of just what the hell was out here, and if things were what they seemed. Admittedly, I also needed the deep breath to steady myself in preparation of what I was about to put myself through.

Gods, this was going to hurt.

"Larry," I whispered. When he appeared, he was dressed for the weather in a very fashionable parka, the fur-lined hood thrown back. "It's not that cold," I chided.

"It felt appropriate, Thomas," Larry responded with a bit of his old snarky self. I forgot how much I missed it. He looked around and shuddered. "Oh. We are here."

"We are," I confirmed. "Do a quick recon of the outside."

The spirit vanished without a word, returning within moments. "Nothing, Thomas. It is quite clear all around, even with the vegetation growing at such an accelerated pace. There is nothing around."

A feeling of déjà vu washed over me. "Anything looks weird, anyone looks like they're coming in here, good or ill, you come to me and tell me," I ordered. "I don't care if it's the denizens of the nine hells, an army of Deadites, or the godsdamned Boy Scouts. You let me know."

"I will, Thomas, on my life." That qualifier was odd coming from the spirit, but things, as I was forced to accept, had changed. Larry wasn't forthcoming with everything that happened in the Time Between, and if he was more vulnerable to harm since he was more visible to others, it made things a bit more difficult.

"No heroics, understand?" When he nodded, I felt something in me twinge with regret. Being at the site was costing Larry as much as it was me. It wasn't right for either of us to be there, but it was necessary. "We'll be out as soon as we can."

Larry nodded again. "Do hurry, Thomas. This place is not right."

"I know." I turned from the spirit and walked to one of the smaller hanger doors, my hands deep in my pockets. I wasn't cold; far from it. I didn't want anyone to see my rage manifest in my hands shaking in utter and complete burning anger. "Come on, you two. You can tell me the story of how the hell you knew I was here while we search the place for clues."

If I didn't know better, it looked like the knee-high grass parted in front of me, allowing me, Rika, and Renton unobstructed access to the hanger door. Considering that the entire place was likely sentient, it wouldn't have surprised me if it did make way. My capacity for accepting surprising events was rapidly expanding, though I didn't expect the vines and kudzu to melt away as it did, pulling away from the doorknob and untangling from the hinges. That was definitely an odd event, though it did make life easier for us to get in.

My left hand came out of my pocket, sweating from the warmth of both the coat and the wrath burning through my blood. I put my hand on the knob and paused. "Places like this are never locked," I whispered, remembering the warehouse, the snow, the wind burning my face. Clamping down on my fear, I threw the door open with a crash and barged in, with Renton right behind me, and Rika covering the rear.

The place was, for lack of a better term, boring. We seemed to have entered the office area of the hanger, which was surprisingly immaculate. The only oddity was the place looked ready for business, but seemed completely untouched. It was like someone came, took everyone, sent a professional cleaning crew in to make the place presentable, and vanished. What made it eerier was the feeling a new group of people were going to come in right behind us and get to work.

"How the hell is this place so clean?" I muttered, my fingers swiping across the metal desk and coming back innocent of dust.

"Like I said, your mother leased the place in perpetuity," Renton said, his voice low. Even he seemed nervous in the quiet. "As this is the place you disappeared, she wanted it kept in case you came back through here. Try to keep up."

As we passed through another office and into a hallway eight feet wide and as many feet high, I slowed. From the way the place looked, the interior had been refurbished into hallways and rooms. Though I knew I never saw the inside of the hanger, that there was a maze in this structure felt like the right answer to me.

"Doesn't explain why it's so clean," I retorted.

"She had agents doing sweeps of the whole building, once a week." Renton sighed. "I would do my own checks, trying to find some clue as to where you went."

I shook my head at the memory of my confinement in another plane of reality. "How did you all find me?" When Renton didn't answer, I turned to face him. In his hand was a touchscreen cell phone with a digital readout of some kind on it. One of the readings was one-point-three meters. A soft, steady series of beeps emanated from the phone's speaker. Realization dawned on me. "Oh godsdammit. Where is it?"

"Implanted between the fourth and fifth vertebrae," Renton said sheepishly. "When you went to the dentist for your fillings."

"When it stopped transmitting, your mom came to us to help her find you," Rika jumped in, and I saw she had her weapon out. Renton's wasn't out, but it was easily accessible. "We ended up here, and found her." I didn't have to ask who the "her" was.

I resumed walking down the hall, trying to keep my emotions in check. Mom had known exactly where I was at all times, except when I went off-world. I was certain she was going to fix that little deficiency in her tracking device before long. "How far?"

"Not much more." Rika came up beside me. "We didn't know what happened. We still don't, not after you left the hospital." I glanced at her and kept walking. "What happened up there?"

"You ever been to Tahiti?" I asked. When she shook her head, I bit off my next words. "It was the exact fucking opposite."

"The hell does that mean?" The Memphis belle was about to drop a bomb on me.

"It means I don't want to talk about it right now," I answered. "Please." Whatever I was going to say next went right out of my head when I turned the corner and saw the body.

It was a surprise to all three of us, coming across a body at all. I jogged the thirty feet to the still form sprawled on the stone floor. The corpse, and it could only be a corpse, looked as if it was tossed contemptuously against the wall after serving its purpose. It was clothed in what was once a button-down shirt, dots and streaks of what looked like chocolate milk but wasn't marring the white cloth. The corpse was facing the wall, obscuring any features. As I stood above the body, I stayed out of the puddle of dried blood it lay in, with no desire to mess up a brand new crime scene.

Granted, it wouldn't have been the first time, but I was trying to turn over a new leaf.

"Friend of yours?" I joked. When both Renton and Rika shook their heads, I took hold of the left sleeve, the one facing the roof. Rika said nothing, telling me they knew either Mom or Renton would handle cleanup. I got a grip on the arm and pulled.

My mind locked at the sight. It wasn't the eyes missing from some rodents taking a munch on the dead man, nor the ruin his face became when the rats ran out of eyes. It wasn't the rictus of the open mouth and the shredded tongue sticking out in pieces. It wasn't even the amount of blood covering the stomach of the corpse. I had been expecting it. It was the source of the blood that made my mind shut down for several moments.

There was a hole in his bare chest, conveniently placed over the heart.

In an instant, I was transported back into the killing chamber, seeing the old madman cutting into Susana's chest. Seeing the gout of blood from the first cut shoot up nearly to the ceiling. The paradoxical look of relaxed concentration on the bastard's face as he kept cutting and breaking and slicing. Seeing his hand reach in and hold her heart to the sky.

I kicked back and scrambled against the wall, horror warring with rage in my head. Renton jumped out of the way as I soundlessly screamed. My breathing came fast and my heart was jackhammering like a machine gun. My chest felt like it was on fire, and my hands covered my heart in reflex and sympathy. I knew those incisions all too well, having seen them up close and personal and in action. It was all too easy to see Susana in that wound.

Both Rika and Renton gave me time to get myself under control, which I appreciated. I took a bit to stop shaking, but I eventually got the anger and fear trapped back in my mind. Out with the bad air, in with the good.

That brought the analytical part of my mind out. Where the hell was the smell? I don't know if you've ever smelled a dead body, but a rotting dead body is one of the worst stenches you could ever smell. It's a primal disgust, since that is what everyone becomes: a decomposing pile of organic matter. Regardless of spirituality, that's where life ended, and it reeked.

At least everything but this body did. It might as well have been covered in neutral Febreeze.

Renton offered me a hand, which I took. That simple act brought me even farther back to my center. Whatever was done to the body kept it either from smelling, which was impossible, or rotting, which ranked in the impossible column as well. Using eyes trained by my mother, I took in everything I could about the corpse.

He stood at over six feet tall, muscles like a bodybuilder. The dark skin was more a grayish hue thanks to exsanguination, or massive blood loss. Ribs were bright white in the dim light, their broken ends jagged and not as accomplished as I had once seen them. Muscle tissue was cut with near surgical precision by a sharp instrument, as was the tissue around the heart. I looked inside the chest cavity and saw blood vessels sliced through like a razor.

I squatted over the poor bastard and patted him down. When I felt the bulge in his back pocket, I knew I had hit jackpot, in more ways than one. That told me another thing. This wasn't a copycat killing, nor was it really an accident finding a body right there, right then. It was a message. Another fucking message.

Once again, they had my complete and undivided attention.

Chapter Three

There are a lot of things I can handle and have handled over the years. Some of them were just little things that were barely more than annoyances, like having a long sharp nasty pointy thing shoved into my thigh, or getting my shoulder dislocated by the physical manifestation of Wrath. Of course, there was also the time I got kicked in the wedding tackle by a Chinese crime lord.

Yeah. Fun times.

However, finding the body of some stranger cut up the same way as my dead wife didn't exactly rank high on the happy-meter. In fact, it was rather the opposite.

Renton had his weapon out, doing a sweep of the hallway ahead, while Rika covered the way we came. I had recovered my composure and cursed that I lost it in the first place. I needed to be better than that; this was when things were going to get dicey, and I could not allow myself to freak out at the tiniest thing. Granted, not many would call finding an eviscerated corpse a tiny thing, but at this point, it was beside the point. Someone left it for me to find, which meant they knew I was back.

I started rifling through his pockets, hearing the clink of change in them. The back pocket had his wallet, which I pulled out and opened. There wasn't much in it besides an expired driver's license, a bank card that had seen better days, and a few business cards that were faded with what looked like several trips through the washer and dryer. The pockets only had change, and no keys. That was interesting in and of itself.

Needing a bit of help, I whispered Larry's name. He appeared instantly, facing away from me. When he turned around, his face, already pale, went waxy. "Oh gods, Thomas. How do you keep getting into these situations?"

"Tell me about it," I muttered. I still wasn't used to everyone being able to see Larry, so I kept my voice low. "You getting anything from this guy?" At Larry's confused look, I clarified. "Something mystical, involving the Conclave, whatever?"

The spirit cleared his throat and narrowed his eyes at the corpse. He then crouched next to me, running his hands over the body. Larry lingered over the hole in the dead man's chest, but only for a moment. It was when he got to the guy's feet that he perked up. "Oh my." To me, Larry said, "There is something about his right foot."

"'Something'? Could you be a bit more vague?" I smiled, trying to take the edge of my words.

"I can do a great many new things, Thomas, but moving material objects is still not one of them."

"Easy, man, it was a joke. Hold on." I moved to the corpse's feet and, careful of the puddle of dried blood, I began taking his shoes off.

Rika chose that moment to return. "What the hell are you doing?"

Without missing a beat, I replied, "Interrogating him."

"What's he going to tell you? 'I've got really bad heartburn'?"

"Larry got a hit from his feet. I want to know what it is." The wallet had fallen to the floor when I moved, and Rika retrieved it. As I pulled his left sock off, I heard a gasp from her.

"Renton!" She hissed the name again, trying to get his attention. When he was close enough, she tossed him the wallet. "Remember this guy?"

The spy caught the wallet with his left hand and read the license. "Horace Pettiford. Now that is rather interesting."

"How?" I struggled to pull the right sock off, which for some reason seemed welded to his foot.

"He stopped by about two weeks ago looking for you," Renton said. "He was rather agitated and adamant that he speak with you."

"That's not the word," Rika interrupted. "Bugshit crazy. That's the better word."

"Those are two words," I muttered absent-mindedly as the sock came off with sudden ridiculous ease. "Well, holy shit."

On poor dead Horace's heel were four Greek letters, the ink several shades darker than his flesh. The letters seemed to glow with a blue light, letting me see them better. "Could you define 'bugshit crazy'? What was he saying?"

"There were people after him, they were trying to kill him, and he needed the Keeper." Renton holstered his weapon as he approached me. "When we told him you were not around, he said he was told you had come back."

"Let me guess: this happened a day before I returned." Renton nodded. "Poor bastard. Larry, my Greek is a bit fuzzy. What's this mean?"

"It says 'Styx'," the spirit answered. "Oh, that is interesting." For the first time, Larry sounded like his old self again. "The ink is made from pomegranates."

"Why is that interesting?" Renton asked.

"Because it fits with the tattoo," Rika put in. "The legend goes that the mother of Achilles wanted her son to never be hurt in battle, so she dipped him in the river Styx. However, she had to hold him by the heel when she dipped him in. He was indestructible unless you hit his heel, then he was fucked."

"Well said, Miss Elder," Larry said with admiration.

I took up the tale. "The pomegranate was used to by the king of the underworld to keep his wife coming back to him. That's why we have seasons." I looked up at Rika. "I'm impressed. When did you get so well-versed in classic Greek mythology?"

Rika looked down at her feet and muttered, "The movies."

It clicked. "You mean *Troy*?" When she flushed, I chuckled. "Oh gods, did that movie suck."

"Four words, Statford: Brad Pitt's naked ass."

I let it go with a visible effort. "Okay, whatever." Looking up and down the hallway, I had a terrible thought. "How often was this place checked?"

"Once a week." Renton paused, then said, "The patrols were stopped after you came back. Otherwise, there'd be one tomorrow."

"They found nothing to report?" Renton shook his head in the negative. "Call Harley. Tell him to get down here with as much luminol as possible."

"Why?"

"Just a hunch." I straightened up from my crouch. "This doesn't bode well." I walked the rest of the way down the hallway, taking a left, then another left, before coming to a door.

"Is this it?" I asked Rika.

Rika nodded. "This is where we found her."

"Yeah." With no more thought, I slammed the door open, the metal ringing throughout the hanger. The scene hit me in the gut like a freight train, because it was almost just like I remembered it. The altar was still there, the blood coating it dried to a copper hue. There were irregular shapes of the same stuff on the stone floor, telling with gruesome accuracy where every one of those psychotic bastards fell after cutting out their own hearts. I heard in my memory's ear the cracking of the ribs, the grunts of exertion, the patter of blood on the floor. Looking up, I saw a large hole in the ceiling above the altar. The metal was twisted and melted, like a flamethrower had hit it. Natural light filtered in through the hole, meaning the blast put a hole in the roof. I had an idea what that might have been, but I would hold my thoughts close on that.

I walked to the slightly raised circle with iron hooks embedded in the stone. "This is where I was." I pointed to the altar. "That's where it happened." It amazed me I could be so calm. There wasn't even any rage in me, which was decidedly odd. "He had me held here, and sacrificed Susana on that altar."

Closing my eyes and seeing the scene again wasn't difficult; it got repeat showings at the theater in my brain every couple of minutes. This time, I stripped out the emotions, doing a little trick I learned in Niflheim of changing the face of the guy strapped to the floor by his arms like something out of a bad old human sacrifice movie. The guy on the floor looked like Horace Pettiford now, which made it easier to deal with.

I took a deep breath and continued, replaying the scene. "After they killed her, they cut me loose, then killed themselves. I don't remember much after that."

"What were you wanting to find here?" Renton asked. Rika was on the phone to Harley Blackwater, still the local medical examiner and chief of crime scene investigations.

"Answers." I let a blanket of pure logic cover my emotions. I needed to separate the feelings from the structure, at least for a little while. "For example, did you find all of her?"

"What do you mean?"

"Her heart. Was it still here?"

Renton looked disgusted. "What kind of question is that?"

"Mister Renton, you are an agent in the employ of my mother, one of the greatest spies in history. You have likely done things in your time before her hiring you that would gag a maggot." My words flowed out like icy rain. "Did you find her heart?"

What I said was like a smack in his face, and I saw the agent in him take over. "We found her, yes, but not her heart." He bit off the words as if they tasted terrible in his mouth. Likely, they did.

"How long did it take you to get here?"

Renton mulled over the answer. "After your mother informed us she had lost contact with your transmitter, it was no more than an hour. The roads were a bit of a problem, since everyone thought it was the end of the world."

"They were right." I looked around, marking the places where the bodies would have been, their positions, and coming to the exact spot Susana breathed her last. "And the rings?"

"Your mother found them off to one side. They weren't well-hidden. The only other thing missing was you."

Variables weren't adding up. One piece was missing, and that was the time between whatever I did and my mom's arrival. An hour may not sound like much, but it can be a lifetime for things to happen.

That was when it hit me.

"Larry, what happened?"

The spirit appeared at the sound of his name, his eyes closed tightly. "Do not make me answer, Thomas." He kept his back to the altar, the color of his coat shifting from cobalt to aqua and all shades in between. "I beg you. Do not make me remember it again."

"I remember it too, Larry."

He rounded on me, his eyes flying open, literal fire burning in the sockets. "You remember only the beginning, Thomas!" Pure venom laced his words. "You were blissfully unconscious while I was but a mewling babe on this godsforsaken floor! I could do nothing but watch them take you. I was useless when they picked you up from under dear Susana."

"Loki got me," I said. "And Him."

"Heimdall and Him," Larry corrected. "They said you were barely sentient," Larry said, the flames in his eyes diminishing to their former clear blue. "Not just alive, but almost little more than a breathing piece of meat. What you did, Thomas…" Larry ran a hand through his hair. "It has never been done before."

"Someone's tried to bring down the gods?"

"No! No one has ever even considered the possibility it could be done." He turned away from me, his arms spreading out to encompass the sacrificial area. "This was nothing anyone could even imagine! Over the years, one or two of the gods may have ended up as mortals, but not at the hands of a mortal and never all at once."

Larry made his way to one of the copper-tinged spots on the concrete. "This is where I hid from those who came." His gaze was riveted to the long-dried blood splatter. "I sank my form into the body of one of the dead cultists as I felt the ones coming were powerful, though not of the power of the Conclave. Little did I know it was two of them, come to collect you."

"What happened then?" I was hungry to know.

"They saw you, covered in her blood." Larry didn't see the wince his words caused. "Heimdall was subdued, and

I believe he knew just how terribly wrong things were."
Larry's form shifted, becoming over a foot taller and wider,
muscles bulging under leather and metal armor. A helmet
formed around his head, horns sticking out well over two feet
in each direction. From his hand a spear appeared, the shaft
at least six inches in diameter and nine feet long. The tip was
golden metal, shimmering rainbows in the light. "She
deserves a proper burial," the faux-Heimdall said, voice
booming. I couldn't tell the difference between the real one
on a bet. "This should not have happened."

Larry shifted again, this time becoming a black man
garbed in a robe of shimmering white and bound about the
waist with a golden cord. The beard was full down to his
chest, the facial hair streaked with silver. There was a
radiance about the man, which Larry mimicked to near-
perfection. It was Him, the god I knew as George. "It did,
and we must make sure nothing happens to him."

Heimdall re-appeared. "And her? She does not
deserve such desecration."

"She does not, but there is little we can do." George's
voice was harsh and practical. I hated it, but understood it.
"We have little time. Get him out of here. Take him where
we discussed. I will deal with loose ends."

"Heimdall left without a word, Thomas," Larry said,
back to his normal self. "When He---"

"George," I interrupted. "I call him George."

Larry raised an eyebrow. "Regardless, He left Susana where she lay, and told me to forget I had seen them. He said you would return when you were well, if you were able." He swallowed hard, fighting back tears, either of rage or regret. "He said I would remember everything when you asked, and not a moment before."

So I had asked, and now had more information, and more questions. I wouldn't learn anything more standing around a former charnel house. The dead still had their secrets, and I had learned very little from this trip down Memory Lane. I knew there was something I was missing, but it kept dancing out of my mind's reach. I let the mask of emotionless thought fall away, the overwhelming sadness threatening to engulf me. I snarled to the mewling in my head to knock it off, that Susana didn't want me crying over her like a kid who just saw Ol Yeller for the first time.

The rage in the back of my mind returned, hammering at the prison around it. I felt it slam against the door, throwing itself against its bonds, beating itself bloody for me to let it loose on something, anything in sight. It wanted to utterly destroy everything and everyone even remotely connected with Susana's murder, and all I was doing was holding it back, which meant it would happily destroy me, too.

I shut that train of thought down quickly. Having two minds was something I had experience with in the not too recent past, and I knew how to keep the two lines of me, the rage and the thinker, merged enough so neither was ascendant. It wasn't two different people; it was two sides of me. I turned down the shrieks in my head and glanced over at Renton.

"Well, that makes things a bit more interesting," I smiled, the gesture feeling plastic on my face.

"The hell do you mean 'interesting?' Why did you come here?" Rika was about to say more, but her phone went off.

Renton nodded at her when she mouthed the word "Harley" at him. "What she means is, why did we come here, Tom?" He put his gun away, seeing there was no longer a need for it. "All we did was bring back old memories."

"Not old for everyone," I muttered. Louder, I continued. "There were parts of the story I was missing. Larry not following me, for one thing. That bugged me. Now I know why." I looked at the spirit. "You have nothing to apologize for, old friend. There was nothing you could do." Before Larry could say anything, I stalked out of the room, and nearly bumped into another blast from the past.

"Bout time you showed up in the real world, asshole." Harley Blackwater was tall, and not in the gangly thin way most people expect when you call someone tall. He was broad across the chest, wide-shouldered, and built like a cross between a long-distance runner and a prize fighter. If I didn't know it was impossible, I would have said he grew another inch or two past the six-three I knew he was. The sharp features, tanned skin, and black hair, which was coarse like raven feathers, screamed his Seneca heritage, and the longer hair tied back and leather pouch hanging from his neck sealed the deal. Harley was an experienced tracker, the medical examiner, the local crime scene investigator for the Hampton/Newport News area, and a friend from the old days. One hand held a gym bag of gear he used for doing his technological CSI magic, and the other held another bag, this one worn leather. It had been years since we talked, and I hadn't even called him to let him know I had reappeared.

That was likely why he pushed past me to talk to Renton. He could hold a hell of a grudge.

"You called, and I came. Where's the body?" Harley's voice rumbled like thunder over the next ridge. He nodded to Larry, which still kind of freaked me out. "Larrisimus. You still hanging around this loser?"

"Hey!" I said, an involuntary laugh coming from me.

Without sparing me a glance, Harley said, "I was talking about Renton. You don't rate that high."

That took me back a bit, and hurt a hell of a lot more than I thought it would. "Wait a godsdamned minute---!"

"No, Tommy, you wait a minute!" Harley whirled on me, dropping the gym bag. "You disappear for two years. I buried a woman and mourned the loss of someone I considered a friend. The entire world goes to hell. I start having long philosophical conversations with things I thought were just abstract fucking concepts." He laughed without any humor. "Hell, I got dating advice from Coyote yesterday. The world finally starts to calm down. People are starting to get a handle on the insanity that is now their day-to-day life.

"And then you show up."

I took a step back from the onslaught. I couldn't say a word.

"You come back to the land of the living without so much as a fucking hello, and expect everyone to follow your lead. Like nothing happened." He snorted at me. "Well, something did happen." Harley reached into the leather sack he still carried and pulled out a long artifact wrapped in tanned hide. It had strips of leather with feathers hanging from a circular design on one end: a medicine wheel. The buckskin was well-worn, looking like it was handed down from the Long Ago to the modern age. It was an actual, honest-to-gods medicine stick, something shamans used in their making of the magic. The feathers looked brand-new, but I knew better than to ask Harley if he'd replaced them. It wasn't the time.

"The magic came back." He pointed the medicine stick at me. I felt the power flowing from it, and was very uncomfortable with the device aimed somewhat at me. "It came back in a big goddamned way. The Great Spirits came back and now they walk Mother Earth and there ain't a fucking thing anyone can do about it." Harley gripped the stick so tightly I was afraid it would snap in his massive hand. Though it creaked, it didn't break. It actually seemed to start glowing in his grasp. "I thought I had buried you along with Susana, and you come back, and don't even give me the decency of a call!" Catching himself, Harley turned from me, muttering under his breath. To Renton, he said, "Get him out of here. I'll give the place a once-over and let you know what I find."

I let myself be guided out of the sacrificial room, trying to find a way to process the hatred Harley poured on me like a monsoon of vitriol. His words hurt me deep, cutting into my soul, and tearing deep furrows in my heart. I admittedly forgot to let him know I was back from the dead; a lot was going on, but that was still no excuse for me not to at least call him and say I was still converting oxygen to carbon dioxide. Things had changed, and I had stayed the same: always leaping before I looked, trying to fight the forces of evil and be just too damned clever for everyone.

In other words, Harley was right. I was an asshole.

Renton seemed to see the desire to apologize in my eyes and put a hand on my chest. "Let him calm down a bit. He had a rougher time than others." I didn't need to be told that Harley did the autopsy; it was plain on the secret agent's face. "He'll be okay. He's been saving that speech for two years."

I smiled slightly, allowing two tears to roll down my cheeks. "He knew I was coming back?"

"No. He had faith you were. Just took longer than he thought." Renton called Rika over. "What did he find out there?"

The cop looked queasy. "I sometimes wish he did it the old-fashioned way." Seeing my blank stare, she explained, "Harley's not just an ME anymore. He's a shaman."

I nodded. "I guessed that from the medicine stick."

"He used the stick to call up the spirits of the people who died in this building," she continued. "There were so many dead," Rika pointed to her chest, "and each one was missing their heart."

"How many?"

"About a hundred."

I started for the exit, my legs stiff as I stalked out of the slaughterhouse. "They covered up what they were doing."

Both Renton and Rika struggled to keep up with me. "What were they doing?" Rika asked my retreating back.

"Godsdammit, though, it makes no sense."

"What makes no sense?"

"What do they need the hearts for?" I stopped so abruptly, the cop and the agent nearly bowled me over. "And why did they just leave him to rot?"

Renton spun me around by the shoulder, igniting a small pain there. "Tom, you need to explain what you're talking about!"

I sighed and resumed leaving the warehouse. There was nothing more for me here, and no reason for us to stick around. I talked rapidly as we went out into the chilled air. It was downtown Newport News, but it smelled like roses compared to the inside of that place of death.

"I'll explain when we get to the office. I need to get a few things, and make a few calls." I tugged on the door handle, willing the damned thing to open.

"Bullshit!" Rika shouted. "You explain it now, or we ain't goin nowhere."

I took a deep breath. When Rika started using that kind of language, she was very slightly on the pissed side. "Look, I promise I'll explain as much as I can guess right now, but only when we get back to the office. Also, I need to make a stop beforehand. There are a few bits I have to iron out in my head first."

"You promise?"

I nodded. "Cross my heart and hope to die," I deadpanned.

The look I got was nothing. The punch to the chest hurt more. I admit, I deserved it, but it was worth it.

Chapter Four

The more things change, the more things stay the same. You would think that, with the world turned inside out and gods and demons doing the Charleston down Main Street every chance they got, someone would stop with useless bureaucracy. It wouldn't take three hours to get a driver's license, because that might be the day one of the various gods of destruction stopped by the DMV to cause a really quick shortening of the line. Traffic would no longer be a nightmare since everyone would get the hell out of the way of the Four Horsemen of the Apocalypse deciding on a roadtrip to see an Ozzy Osbourne show in Topeka. That would be about twenty levels of awesome, and almost worth having the gods down on the mortal plane, as annoying as the bastards could be.

Instead, I found out some things never change.

"Eight hundred dollars," I muttered.

We were in my office again, this time with me behind my desk, and my handlers seated in the chairs next to the couch. On my desk was my new phone, which was comfortably ensconced in a case adding three times its weight to protect the device. It was a long time since I owned a phone. I mused I could likely use it for both body armor and hand-to-hand combat if it came down to it.

Renton was unsympathetic. "You were the one who wanted the latest version of your old phone." He stretched out in his chair, and I heard bones cracking in his shoulders. "And of course, there's inflation to take into account."

"Still a bit of a shock," I mused, plugging the device into my laptop. Not so incredibly, the damned thing still worked. It's always a good thing to have people around who will use your place when you disappear into the ether; they take care of the place while you're a mad god's plaything.

"What are you doing?" Renton asked. He glanced at Rika, who was checking her own phone.

"I've been out of it for a while, but not too long to remember how to restore the data from my old phone." With the click of a button, two-year-old information began to get written in the magic memory chip. "I'm smarter than I look."

"Doubtful." Rika murmered.

Renton chuffed out air in disbelief. He had let me hear a couple of earfuls, and likely was going to give me another, but Rika beat him to it. "What were we doing there?"

I sighed, frustration coloring my words. I knew my attempt at deflecting questions with shiny electronics wouldn't work, but it was worth a try. "I told you: I needed to see, and I needed to know. No more, no less." I pulled out some paper and a pen and began to write. "You may think I don't know what I'm doing, but I have a plan."

"What the hell kind of plan is it to have one of your best friends show up in a slaughterhouse?" Rika put her phone inside her jacket. "You know he was the one who did the post-mortem." She paused for effect. "On all of them."

That stung my soul. Harley was truly one of the best people I could ever know; being there could not have been any easier for him than me. I swallowed down the pain and continued writing. "It wasn't my intent."

"That's your only saving grace in this, Tom," Renton jumped in. "You don't know any better anymore. This is not the world you left."

"I didn't leave on purpose." I snapped.

"Be that as it may, you did." Renton stood, crossing his arms over his broad chest. "This is not a normal world anymore. Things have changed so much you can't possibly understand." He glared at me. "And you certainly won't understand them hiding in this office."

His words hurt me deeply as I wrote a few more words on the paper, my penmanship looking like a cross between a kidnapper and a meth addict. It would have to do. "You're right. I don't understand everything going on." I put the pen down and massaged my forehead. "I'm trying to get back some of the life I had before I was taken away. I have to do that, or I'll---"I cut myself off, my eyes slipping shut at the memory, the scent of disinfectant, the feel of needles in my arms, the sight of a flame-haired brute stalking for my life.

"You'll what?" Rika walked to my desk. I could hear the concern in her voice. As much as I wanted to give in to the idea of giving up, I didn't need concern.

I needed steel.

"Nothing." My voice hardened, my ball of regretful rage denied release once again. My mind ordered up what I needed. "Harley likely won't talk to me for a good while. Can you ask him to find out more about the dead there? Who they were, what they did, all that. There's something there, or should be there. There has to be a connection."

I could see the look of poorly veiled disgust on her face. "What happened to you?" Rika demanded suddenly. "What the hell happened to you? You were never this cold."

"I can't think about that now." I put the papers in my coat. "I have to focus."

"One of these days, you're going to have to talk about it." Rika shook her head as she grabbed up her own coat. "I'll run your little errand, but we're going to talk about this. We're your friends; we don't deserve to be kept in the dark."

Before I could come up with something to say, she left, the door barely staying in the frame as it slammed closed. She needn't have bothered; she could have stood there all day and I wouldn't have been about to say anything, or at least nothing she would accept. I didn't lie to her; there was a plan.

"Larry?" I waited for him to appear, then said, "I need a lead. Something. Anything."

"I do not know what to tell you, Thomas. I have nothing."

To Renton, I said, "You have anything?"

"This tattoo on the corpse's ankle means something, but I don't know what it means. A lot of cults have popped up. Even though the gods aren't as cosmic as they once were, they have quite a bit of power."

"And I doubt they know a damned thing about what happened." George and Loki had likely only been ahead of the chaos by minutes, which meant questioning any of the rest of the Conclave was completely useless. "I need someone who's got some knowledge about what's going on," I paused in remembering, "and who can tell me why so many of the Conclave decided to settle down right here."

Renton took his keys out of his pants pocket. "I can answer the second part of that question, and I'm surprised you don't know it. The first part of that can be answered by an old friend of yours. Come on."

We left my office, Larry in tow, Renton up front. "An 'old friend'?" I wracked my brain for a name. "I got nothing."

Renton sighed. "You have been gone too long, Tom." He glanced sidelong at me as we got into his musclecar. "You aren't who you were." When I opened my mouth to say something, he held up his hand. "I know: you lost Susana. Right in front of you, even. It was and is a terrible thing."

The rage I kept bottled in my head wanted to pounce. I knew Renton could disembowel me with his bare hands if he desired, and that knowledge was just enough to assuage my anger. "Yeah, it is." I bit off each word as if they were bitter poison.

"It always will be." Renton started the car with a roar. "What you are doing, however, is pushing away those who would help you in some crazed quest for vengeance." He backed up out of the parking space and pulled out of the lot, the engine uttering such a growl I thought a nearby Honda would jump onto the sidewalk with fear. "You don't have to do this by yourself."

I let my breath out in a rush. My rage flowed out with the exhale. "Let me play this close to the vest for a bit, Renton. I have my reasons, and you would understand them if I told you."

We drove in silence for several miles before I saw our destination. In the meantime, I went over my thoughts of the situation, such as it was.

That someone wanted me out of the way was a given; apparently more than one group of people wanted me out of the way, as the cultists were one faction, and George and Loki represented another faction, this time involving the gods, or at least concerned members of the Conclave. That there were likely other folks who had plans to get me out of play was a given; it just wasn't clear who had nefarious or altruistic reasons for such actions. I always considered some of the gods to have some redeeming features, but I couldn't count on that for all of them. It was likely they were looking just to save themselves and if I could be salvaged, so much the better.

That left me with a series of questions. First: who were the cultists, the ones who carved out hearts? Who had set them on my trail? Someone had popped the idea of their flavor of Armageddon into their heads, and put me as the cause of, and the solution to, all their problems of a non-destroyed world. They were very slick, very capable, and, most disturbingly, very dedicated to their cause. Of course, they were also supposed to be very dead.

Second question was, who was doing the job on those corpse after I went out of the blue and into the black? Horace might not have been a Navy SEAL or anything of that nature, but he wasn't a small man, and likely would have made more of a mess out of things trying to get away. There were no defensive wounds, nor did he have anything that looked like scraped flesh under his fingernails. The idea the cultists survived their own suicide scared the hell out of me.

It also went right out the window the more I thought about the damage to the body. My mind went back to the wound. It was sloppy, with no real style or care about the cut.

The heart was probably all but torn from the chest, with little more thought than getting the organ out of the ribcage as quickly as possible. Something like that was directly opposed to the relative elegance of the operations I saw two years before.

The cultists were artists; this was the work of a rank amateur.

The third question: Why leave the body out at all? Other than the message it sent, that someone was still doing unspeakably horrific acts in a place that had gone from warehouse to slaughterhouse, whoever was behind it kept the place neat and tidy, until a week prior to my visiting. The only difference between then and now was stark and obvious: I had returned. It was pretty amazing what the presence of one person could cause.

Speaking of one person, my jaw dropped at the sight of where we were headed. I think a couple of squeaks came out of me as Renton pulled into an open visitor spot. The shit-eating grin on Renton's face was almost more than I could actually stand. When I finally found my voice, I was as calm and rational as anyone would expect me.

"Why the living hell are we at the cop shop?" I pointedly refused to unbuckle my seatbelt.

"Like I said, we're here to talk to an old friend." Renton was maddeningly sublime, his voice barely above conversational.

I looked out the window at the Hampton/Newport News Police Headquarters building. It was a stone edifice that looked more like a turn-of-the-century hospital, which kind of made sense, as it actually was. The granite was weathered and worn, the color of rolling storm clouds. Windows were spaced with military precision, though their order of lighting was at best haphazard. From the few lights I saw, and the general lack of vehicles in the parking lot, the local constabulary was otherwise occupied doing gods knew what.

"Oh come on, man," I muttered. "You know I'm just about as *persona non grata* as I can get around here without getting a set of matching bracelets. Why would you bring me here?"

Renton reached down and unbuckled my seatbelt. The belt slid across my chest to its resting spot above my right shoulder. "Because you are out of touch." He got out of the car and walked over to the passenger side. After he opened the door, he smiled again. "Because you are not in as complete control as you think you are." With a steel grip on my right arm, he gently but firmly guided me out of the car. "And because, in spite of what you think, or what you think you know, you still have friends here. Good friends who will go to the mattresses for you."

His choice of words was odd, but I understand what he meant. I had cultivated a good relationship with everyone in the local police force as best I could. More to the point, I made sure I didn't piss off anyone any more than necessary. Most of that was to keep Susana out of a bad position, but even before she and I got together, I was good friends with most of the boys and girls in blue.

Most, that was, except for Chief Parkinson.

Parkinson was a climber, plain and simple. He was also the Chief of Police, the Top Cop, for the Hampton/Newport News area, which covered a hell of a lot of real estate. Parkinson also had his fingers into every single shady and quasi-legal deal he could that wouldn't land him behind bars. I have no idea how he got the job in the first place; the dirt he had on those above him must have been of epic quality. When I went missing, he was in talks to go for state senator, and I wondered how that turned out. It would have been a huge change, though I imagined he would have plenty of pull regardless what job he wrangled. Parkinson was a bully, plain and simple, with a bull head and piggish eyes that seemed to be the standard uniform for bullies the world over.

And it looked like Renton was taking me to see him.

The trip through the back door of the building was one I had taken many times, not always without handcuffs. With the way the place was built, there was little to no chance of the interior changing. We passed the entrance to the holding cells, and I could smell something coming from that hallway, a scent of jasmine. It was so strong as to be almost cloying. I made a mental note to check that out later; plants don't smell that strong unless you're covered in them or someone boosted them. Old habits died hard.

Renton led me up the back stairs, away from the bustle of the booking area. I could almost see the wall throb from the volume of voices on the other side. Voices of every kind were in the mix: old, young, male, female, scared, belligerent. The only thing they had in common was they wanted help. I heard the pleading underlying every word, every syllable, as we made our way up to the squad room.

When we entered the squad room, it was almost like I had never left. The desks were in the same places, the chairs looked almost as old as the building, and the newest things there seemed to be the computers. Those near the doorway looked up as Renton pushed me along. Silence spread across the room as the other detectives and sergeants saw me. Soon, I had everyone's attention. I nodded to several of the cops, both plain-clothes and uniformed, seeing those I remembered from the old days, and those who were too new for anything but the tales of the crazy detective who actually wasn't that crazy. A couple of the detectives came up and offered muted condolences. I couldn't remember their names off-hand, but they looked much older than the last I saw them. Two years? It looked more like a decade or more.

I thanked them through numb lips as Renton kept us going inexorably towards the Chief's office. The secretary was new, but then, Parkinson changed them out as often as he could. Renton smiled at her, an older lady with grey hair, very different from the bubbly, bubbleheaded blondes Parkinson preferred. I was about to say something when Renton interrupted me.

"Is the Chief in, Denise?" He clapped me on the shoulder. "I have someone who needs to see him."

"Of course, Mr. Renton," she answered, chipper and sounding like a girl fresh out of high school. "He's been looking forward to this."

"Yeah, I'll bet he has," I muttered.

Denise picked up the handset on her phone and said a few words. "Go on in. He'll see you now."

As we walked to the door, I whispered to Renton, "Why are we wasting time here? I don't have any friends here."

Renton was silent as he pushed open the door to the inner sanctum of the office of the Chief of Police. Adorning the walls were trophies, pictures of dignitaries and politicians, and some diplomas. There were the usual bookshelves containing books that would never be read, the typical monolithic desk that looked carved from a single block of wood, and the two leather and metal chairs in front of the desk were guests would sit in audience to the Chief.

The chair behind the desk looked like the back of a throne, turned away from the desk and the occupant looking out the window at the cold grey sky. Knowing Parkinson like I did, that's exactly what we were in for: an audience with a godsdamned king.

So, resigned to my fate, I strode forward and plopped down in one of the chairs. Renton was more sedate in his seating. Parkinson was no fan of mine, nor I him. Why should that change?

"Well, you've waited this long for me to come to you for help," I said, my voice boisterous and full of false cheer. "Here I am."

For a moment, nothing happened. I wondered for a moment if anyone actually was in the chair when it slowly began to turn around. I was about to let loose a few choice words when my jaw dropped to somewhere near my chest.

"Oh you have got to be kidding me." It was the only thing I could get out.

"Kept me waiting, huh?" James MacPherson, Chief of Police, said with a smile on his face.

It's not often I'm left speechless. This was one of those times. Mark your calendars, folks.

Chapter Five

Two years is a hell of a long time. It's a full term of a Congresscritter. It's half a term for President. Your average phone or computer is ancient in that amount of time, and most television shows are little more than a memory.

I had lost so much in two years. My wife, my family, my friends. I had even lost nearly the entire time itself putting myself back together after getting taken apart by some cosmic lightshow. I lost the world I knew, the gods turning my home into their playground. For years, things were taken from me. Finally, I got something back.

My best friend.

When I could talk again, I spouted off my rapier wit. "Mac? The fuck are you doing here?" See? Sharp as pudding.

James MacPherson, a lieutenant of no small reputation, was sitting back in his overstuffed leather chair and smiling broadly. His high-cut blonde hair had a few flecks of silver in it, somehow giving him more respectability than he had before. Sky-blue eyes twinkled behind bifocals, the thin frames a no-nonsense black. Mac's dark blue suit was one of those tailored jobs, cut with his wiry frame in mind. There were a few more lines on his face, especially around the mouth and eyes, trying to draw him into a permanent scowl. The job of being chief of police could do such, of that I had no doubt. The sunny grin, however, nearly dispelled the aging, making my old good friend look years younger.

"I finally got one over on you, Tom," Mac laughed. He looked at Renton and nodded. "He had no idea?"

The agent smiled. "Not a clue. He thought your predecessor was still around."

Mac's face darkened at the mention of Parkinson. "That horrible excuse for a human being. Be glad he's not in this chair anymore, Tom," Mac said. "He was working on making you disappear."

"Someone else was already doing that, Mac." My own voice was low and gruff. Trying to change the subject, I faked a smile. "'To the mattresses'," I chuckled. "I must be getting old. I didn't even get the reference."

"You are, but you've been through more than most." Mac leaned forward, his fingers laced together and hands resting on his desk. "I'm so sorry about Susana. What happened to her was inhuman."

I nodded brusquely, keeping my mind from focusing on the gaping hole in her chest, the cavity that no longer held her heart, the lungs pink and glistening, blood spurting from the aorta in fits. "Yeah, it was." It was all I could say without tears threatening to flow. The pain was still too raw to intellectualize for long periods of time, and I felt it being rubbed like an exposed nerve on a belt sander.

"We've pretty much figured out the sequence of events," Mac said, trying to remain businesslike. "We've also figured out a few things about the cultists."

"The cultists?"

"Yeah. Thanks to your mom and Mister Renton, we found they were all members of the same family from a tribe in the Yucatan." Mac reached down and opened a drawer. There was a rattle as he pulled out a folder at least three inches thick. When he set it down in front of him, he exhaled heavily. "This is everything we have on them. Unfortunately, the majority of the paperwork is autopsy reports, each one almost perfectly identical."

"All the reports are in there?" My voice was tightly under control.

Mac caught my meaning. "Not all of them. Just the cultists."

"What else did you find?"

Renton interjected. "Not a lot. We know where they came from, but not how they got into the States, nor how they managed to sneak that altar into that warehouse."

Mac nodded enthusiastically. "Yeah! That thing weighs a few tons, heavier than it looks, and according to the guys at the lab, it's well over fifteen hundred years old." He shook his head as he read from a pink sheet of paper. "Every museum in ten countries was fighting for a look at it. You should have seen the standoff between the museum guys from Guatemala, the Smithsonian, London, and Mexico. I thought it was going to turn into a nerdfight at the warehouse."

"What happened?" I was drawn into the story in spite of myself.

"Your mother," Renton smiled. "They all pleaded with her to let them take it with them. She told them no."

I was flabbergasted. "That's it? That's all she said?"

"It wasn't what she said," Mac said, "so much as how she said it." When my face registered confusion, he clarified. "She had the head curator of the Smithsonian by the throat when she said it. Requests to even see the thing vanished overnight."

"Yeah, that sounds like her," I nodded. I could see the entire event in my head without a problem. My mom wasn't one for empty threats, and there was a very lucky man in the form of the curator who got to breathe another day. If I knew her, and I'd like to think I did, she put the fear of the gods into every sane person on earth.

That meant whoever killed all those people was decidedly insane. What an unexpected surprise.

"So do you have anything for me, Mac?"

The chief of police, my friend, looked pained as he closed the folder. "No. Those cultists were out of nowhere, and even if they weren't, there likely isn't anything to find anyway."

"Mac---" I began.

"Tom, you don't understand what happened. You know why Parkinson isn't around anymore?" Mac didn't let me answer. "It was a forced retirement, Tom. He didn't have a choice in the matter." My stupid look must have been showing again, because Mac rolled his eyes and leaned forward. "He was told to get the hell out by this guy." He tossed a small medallion over to me.

I caught it in mid-air, but I didn't need to see it; I knew who the patron saint of cops was. We had met before. "So Michael told him the gig was over. I didn't know he took that much interest in mortal affairs."

Mac laughed at that. "He's putting Internal Affairs out of business!" The mirth died quickly. "Sounds like a good thing, yeah? The problem is, we lost nearly half the force." Mac sat back in his chair again, rubbing his chin. I heard the stubble scraping his hand like sandpaper. "Michael didn't have to tell them all to bail; they took it upon themselves for the most part to be successful somewhere else. That hurt us badly."

"How long ago was that?" I asked.

"About six months after you vanished. It was pretty bad around here. I got the job by default, mainly because I knew you." Mac gave a lopsided smile. "About time palling around with you paid off."

"So in a year and a half, you're not back to strength?"
I was somewhat disbelieving and more than a bit
disheartened.

"No, we have the people. It's the experience we don't
have." The chief of police stood up and went to his window.
"I lost another ten percent of the force when things really got
weird." He shoved his hands in his pockets past the wrist, a
move that told me he was trying to hide his shaking hands.
Whether from reliving the anger or fear of the time he was
remembering, I couldn't know. "How do you tell the mayor,
the governor and several high-ranking military guys that not
only was it a bad idea to shoot the large serpent that came out
of the sky and vanished into the sea, but it could start the end
of the world." Mac exhaled heavily. "I remember the comic
books, even if he wasn't big enough to go around the world."

Jormundgundr, the Midgard Serpent was around. That
just filled me with all sorts of wonderful warm fuzzy
feelings, kind of the way a sulfuric acid enema would. "Good
call on that. He doesn't enjoy dealing with mortals much, and
with gods even less. He's a sign of the end of the world, you
know."

"Yeah, I know." Mac turned to face me, his eyes
looking older. "We got a bunch of those the first few months.
And by a bunch, I mean just about all of them. Thankfully we
didn't see a creature with seven heads and horns or whatever.
I can't remember which right now, but I probably would

have lost just about everyone else from that one." He put a hand on the back of his chair and closed his eyes for a moment, seeming to take strength from the wood and leather seat. "It was a really bad time, Tom."

"Because he is a friend, your mother offered assistance," Renton said. I jumped a little, as I genuinely forgot he was in the room. That man was scary in his ability to disappear in plain sight. "Needless to say, he jumped at the chance, and your mother made sure no one went off half-cocked. There was talk of starting at nukes and working up from there. It was a rough time for everyone."

"That's putting it very mildly. I did everything I could do to keep things together. Your mom helped, but at the end of the day, I was the cheese that stood alone." Mac sat back down, his shoulders hunched over. He straightened up after a moment. "But you're back now. That makes things a touch better." Mac smiled at me. "It has to make it better."

I crossed my arms in front of me, then put them in my coat pockets. I didn't think I would see Mac so soon after returning, so this was a bit of a surprise; I thought I'd have to seek him out. This both complicated things and made them easier. "Mac," I began, "I'm on the hunt for someone, and I can't be distracted from it right now."

His face fell almost comically. "Distracted? The entire world has been invaded by powered-down gods and uppity demons and you don't want to get 'distracted?' What the hell is that supposed to mean?" Mac placed his hands flat on his desk. "I need your help, man! I'm so far out of my depth I can't even see the shore!"

"You've done pretty well without me so far, Mac." I pulled my hands from my pockets as I stood. "In fact, you've done a hell of a job without me."

"Do you know how many different gangs are out there? Each one dedicated to a different god?" Mac ran a hand through his hair. "I don't know the differences between them all, and negotiating that diplomatic minefield is like running across a full firing range blindfolded. I need you, Tom."

I gave a tight smile. "You've done great for two years."

Mac shook his head. "I've been holding on by my fingernails. Now that you're back, I'm either going to fall all the way off or---"

"Or I'll keep you hanging on, Mac," I completed. "I just need a few days to tie up some loose ends."

Something in my tone must have caught his attention. "That doesn't sound very encouraging."

"No?"

"For you, tying up loose ends puts insurance companies into bankruptcy and area hospitals into overdrive."

I couldn't argue with him on that. "When the time comes, Mac, I'll be there. I just have to finish something."

From the look in Mac's eyes, I could see he knew what I needed to finish. "Okay, Tom, and when the time comes, I'll be there, too. Just say the word."

I laughed as Renton stood and followed me to the door. "Be careful what you say, Mac. I might just take you up on it."

Mac and I said our goodbyes, and Renton and I left One Police Plaza in silence. The roar of Renton starting his car filled the air, dropping to a low mutter as he let it idle. He drummed his fingers on the steering wheel, not looking at anything. If I had to guess, Renton was waiting for me to have some brilliant idea on where to go since going to the cops accomplished about ten percent of nada.

Truth be told, I didn't think going to the police would do anything anyway. I had planned on visiting the local precinct to find Mac anyway, but I didn't think they'd have any information I could use. Finding Mac, especially in his elevated position, was a bonus of excellent proportions, and I had to do some quick recalculating.

The thing was, no matter how I changed the numbers, they all added up to blood and pain.

"I know you're waiting for where we go now, Renton," I said. "I've been thinking."

"Dangerous," he responded.

"Ass. And I have an idea."

"Doubly dangerous." His deadpan delivery made me laugh in spite of myself.

"It's a long trip. I'll need a plane to get there quickly." The more I thought about it, the more I wondered why I didn't think of it earlier.

"That's the easy part," Renton said, pulling the car out of the parking space and setting us on the road. "Where are we going?"

"In all the excitement of coming back, I forgot a few things." I pinched the bridge of my nose; I felt a tension headache coming on. "First things first: back to the office. I need to pack a couple of things."

"And then?"

I clenched my jaw for a moment. "I have manners to make, and a favor to call in."

"Also, you're saying 'I' a lot, Tom." Renton gave me a sideways glance. "You are going nowhere without me." When I opened my mouth to protest, he cut me off. "That's not just my idea. Your mother wants an eye on you at all times."

"You're my babysitter?" I laughed out of reflex.

"I'm the one who's supposed to keep you safe. Call it babysitting all you want, but it's my job to keep you from getting killed unnecessarily."

"As opposed to necessarily?"

Renton took his eyes off the road long enough to give me a scathing glare. "You know what I mean, Tom. I'm stuck to you at the hip, whether you like it or not."

That put a kink in my plans, but I had taken such probabilities into account after I got back. Well, if he was going to be on my back for a while, then he would have to keep up. "Okay, Renton, you want to ride the crazy train, you better hold on to your butt. It's going to be a bumpy ride."

"You obviously haven't seen some of the places I've gone with your mother," Renton muttered while pulling out a small earpiece. A few muffled words later, he said, "The plane will be ready when we get there. Only question is where are we going?"

"I need to see someone who owes me a solid. Before that, though…" I paused, covering my face with my hands and taking a deep breath.

After a silence, Renton cleared his throat. "Before that?" He prompted.

I pulled my hands away and put them in my pockets. That metallic lump was still there. "I have to talk to the Don." I smiled at Renton, who looked slightly green with the prospect. "Still want to tag along?" Renton's response was rather predictable.

"Should I bring extra ammo or body armor?"

Chapter Six

Flying in the brave new world was actually a lot like it was before the Fall. You get a flight plan, you file it, and you take off for your destination. Sometimes you lose your luggage, sometimes you're early, and usually you're late.

Of course, there were differences. I mean, you never heard pilots report a flock of angels at thirty-five thousand feet, or a flight of dragons cruising along at just above cloud level. Then there were the flying carpets, the brooms, the ones who just said forget it and flew on their own power...

You know what? Forget what I said. Flying was absolutely and completely different save for one major detail: it was still a pain in the ass.

After packing a couple days clothes, Renton and I made our way to the airport with very little issue. The takeoff was delayed thanks to scheduling problems in the form of a dragon, specifically Ao Run, the Dragon King of the West Sea. He had stopped in for a bite to eat before heading for his temple in Oregon, and was upset he had to wait for a medical plane to take off. We knew this because he bellowed his displeasure across the tarmac for all to hear.

You've heard of first world problems? These were new world problems.

We took off in the late evening and landed only an hour later by the clock. A Gulfstream V can really move when it needs to, and I had no doubt my mom made sure she had the best airplane the government could afford. The ride was fairly smooth, with only a couple of course corrections to dodge a phoenix and a firebird who crossed our path.

A note: Don't ever ask what the difference is. They can be a bit touchy about it.

We touched down in Brownsville/South Padre Island Airport just before sundown. The airport was modern enough, meaning I didn't worry about electricity or hot and cold running water. However, the moment we were out of the plane, I saw I had not more than two bars of service on my phone, and the only available wireless was from the plane. There was also no terminal. Instead there was a building about a half-mile away from the plane where we walked to get out of the not-unusual Texas heat. No tram, no cart for the luggage, just beating feet over a scorching runway bleeding off the last of the day's heat.

First world problems.

The car was a current-year Honda, a new model called a Ryu, It was a simple two-door vehicle that according to the rental place got great gas mileage for an affordable price. It looked so much like an old AMC Gremlin, I thought Renton would apoplexy, but he went along with it as the only other thing was a late-model Dodge that brought a look of utter horror to the secret agent's face.

As we drove to the Don's estate, I mulled over all the possible things I could say, and they all came up as useless hollow excuses. I promised the man I would protect his daughter, and I failed in possibly the most spectacular way possible. Don Salvador Iglesias y Marquez was not a man to disappoint or a man to cross. Before I met him, and before Susana became a cop and involved with me, Don Salvador was the Mexican version of the Godfather. He ran every illicit and illegal thing north and south of the border. From smuggling to contract murder, the Don had his hand with it. The only thing he never did was human trafficking, which was at least something. After Susana and I got married, he reportedly went legit, getting rid of his smuggling operations and toning down on the killings. The Don became a protector of the border, from Brownsville, Texas to San Ysidro, California, and all places in between. He was an average-looking man, around my height but more wiry. The last I saw him, the silver had yet to take over the black in his hair. His power was in his eyes, though. One moment, they were full of life and happiness, and all was right in the world.

When they went dark, that was when it became time to make peace with whatever god you worshipped, and asked them for mercy, because the Don would show you none.

Renton was the first to break the silence. "You sure you're okay for this, Tom?"

"No, but it's necessary and the right thing to do." I was picking at the crappy upholstery on the seat. "I have to face the music for what I did."

"Oh, yes, shame on you for getting kidnapped," Renton responded dryly. "As you said it wasn't my fault for what happened to you and Susana---"

"Sorry for costing you that hundred, by the way," I smiled.

"---You are not at fault for getting abducted by whatever took you." The spy tapped his fingers on the steering wheel. "I'm certain Don Salvador will understand what happened and you weren't to blame."

"Hundred bucks says someone tries to kill us there." The words were out of my mouth before I could take them back.

"You're on," Renton accepted without hesitation. "I remember the Don being very reasonable and clearheaded. Granted, this was before what happened to Susana, but even then, I don't think he holds you at fault."

"I made the man a promise, Renton," I said, "and I broke it. Whether I'm the one who did it or someone else did it, the fact is I broke my word to him."

Renton shook his head, whether in disagreement or amusement, I have no idea. On our right was the University of Texas Rio Grande, a sprawling complex of buildings that broke up the landscape with labs and student housing. It was all very normal and boring, which was likely why the Don lived near it. There were young folks everywhere, students most likely, though there were a few people who seemed too perfect to my eyes. They weren't a threat, but they weren't normal, mundane mortals, either. That brought a question to my mind: what else did the Fall cause? Did it change the regular people? What else could be blamed on me?

I shook those thoughts away as we made a left onto River Levee Road, which according to the GPS was the road the Don's estate was located. The foliage on the sides of the two-lane street was a gorgeous verdant green, almost like you'd expect drops of paint to come off the leaves and branches. There was a clean smell to the place, making me want to keep the windows down. It was nature, something I missed in the hustle and bustle of city life. The car was going only twenty, but the scent had no problem getting in. A golf course was to our right, which I figured the Don either owned outright or at least had a controlling interest. To the left was a strip of wild growth, and just beyond that was the Rio Grande. After that was Mexico, which I had no interest in visiting for a good while.

About a mile down the road, the Don's estate loomed. Perched on the border between two nations, it was actually pretty sedate. There was a third floor visible above the privacy wall, but it looked only capable of holding a bedroom as small as it was. The wall was a dozen feet tall at least, and I could see the twinkle of either glass or sharp metal in the fading sun. Knowing the Don, it was probably both. The roof was slate, with flat solar panels in addition to the shingles. Two chimneys jutted toward the sky. The wall blocked off the rest of the place, but from the pictures Susana had shown me, I knew the place was nearly nine thousand square feet.

Okay, so it was sedate for the rich folks.

Renton asked the obvious question as we approached the front gate at a crawl. "Does he know we're coming?"

"I didn't tell him. I didn't want to have to try explaining myself over the phone. Odds are, though, he knows we're here. Not many Gulfstreams come in to Brownsville that don't belong to him, I imagine. He's had eyes on us since before we set down."

"I figured. How do you want to play this?"

I grit my teeth and set my jaw firmly. "Like he's my father-in-law and I'm begging his forgiveness for the death of his daughter."

Renton shrugged. "Playing it straight. I can go along with that."

My voice was incredulous. "You're going to have to! Gods, man, does everything have to be a firefight with you?"

The spy brought the car to a stop at the gate, where a young man stood cradling a submachine gun. "If it looks like a duck, Tom."

"Out of the car, please." The gate guard looked in his mid-twenties and was dressed at odds with the heat and humidity in a suit and tie. His black hair was cut short and his eyes were covered in a pair of aviator shades. The Uzi hanging from a strap on his right shoulder was well-oiled and looked well-maintained. Another guard came out of the small building attached to the gate, almost a mirror image, down to the Uzi and sunglasses.

Renton switched off the car and slowly opened the door. I opened my side and stood, my back creaking slightly from having sat for so long. "We're here to see Don Salvador," I said, placing my hands on the roof at the guard's gesture.

"Lots of people want to see Don Salvador, *señor*." I felt hands under my arms, at my waist, and ankles. "Why should he want to see you?"

"Just so you know, I'm armed," Renton said as the second guard moved behind him.

"Thank you for your honesty," he said. His voice was lower than the first guard's, with a bit of gravel to it. The guard pulled out Renton's Desert Eagle and placed it on the roof of the Ryu. To his partner, he said, "Clear."

"Now, why are you here to see the Don?" Guard One gently turned me around to face him.

"I'm his son-in-law."

Not surprisingly, that got us inside in less than two minutes. Passing the gate showed off the rest of the house, the second floor slightly smaller than the first. The architecture was beautiful, though I could see signs of security everywhere, which brought down the serenity of the place. The walls were a mixture of brick and stucco, with the former making up more of the construction. Bushes and small tracts of flowers followed the sidewalk and driveway all the way up, the blooms bursting with color. Even though it was the middle of winter, everything was vibrant and alive.

I can't say I was ready to head into the lion's den, but I knew it had to be done. There were things that needed to be said, and I couldn't hide behind the excuse of being on another plane of reality or the other side of the country. A sense of finality settled over me. I had to do this, not just for myself, but for the ghost of my life before I vanished.

That doesn't mean, of course, I wasn't scared shitless when our escort pulled the double doors to the study open.

Seated in an overstuffed leather chair, facing a roaring fire, was the Don himself. He had his legs crossed, and a small crystal tumbler under his left hand. I could see him in profile, and what I saw was a man looking ten years older than the last I saw him. The goatee was almost pure silver and there were more lines on his face. It broke my heart seeing him, a man filled with energy and life, so aged. His clothing looked big on him, like it would act as a sail in a strong breeze, blowing him away into the night.

Renton looked fairly relaxed, even though we were surrounded by a few more guards, all armed, all cocked, locked and ready to rock. I wasn't too worried, either, as if things went pear-shaped, it wouldn't be the guards killing me. That honor would belong to the Don, if he wished it.

I took a moment to take in the study. The room was paneled in solid mahogany, the bookshelves full of classics I had no doubt were the originals. There were a great many pictures, all framed, some hanging on the wall, some in little stand-up frames. I tried to keep the pain from my mind when I saw a photograph of Susana, her head thrown back in laughter, from our first summer as man and wife. There were no windows into the room; the only light came from the fire and the lamps unevenly spaced across the study. It was dim, but I could pick out all the fine details. There was only one exit, and we were in front of it.

My Spanish was pretty terrible, but I caught the gist of the guard's brief exchange with the Don, who dismissed everyone with a wave of his hand. Renton and I stood where we were as the doors closed behind us. There was a loud click as the guards locked the door behind us. That is rarely a good sign.

I opened my mouth to say something, but the Don held up a hand, silencing me before I could speak. Instead, he broke the silence, his rough voice cracking. "I was expecting you earlier, Thomas."

"Yes, sir," I said simply.

"My daughter is dead."

"Yes, sir."

"Did you do anything to try and stop it?"

My own voice broke, tears welling in my eyes. "I swear to you, on her name, I did everything I could to save her."

"On her name, Thomas? Why not your own life?"

"Because my life ended the day hers did, Don Salvador." I couldn't trust my voice anymore after a brief sob escaped, and I covered my eyes with my hands.

When I removed my hands from my face, the Don stood in front of me. His own eyes were filled with tears, and he looked at me with a sad smile. "My son, I know you did all you could. It wasn't your fault." He pulled me close in an embrace, arms around me. I returned the hug, and the tears fell on his shoulder. I whispered to him how sorry I was, how I never meant for anything to happen to her, how I even sent her away to keep her safe. The Don nodded, answering my begging his forgiveness with his acceptance.

The Don led me to a couch and sat me down. To Renton, he asked for a glass of water. "You came here expecting me to kill you, Thomas?"

I took a slow drink of the cool liquid, the ice clinking in the glass. "I can't say I would have blamed you."

"Two years ago, you would have been right," the Don said, sitting back in his chair. I looked at him and saw a bit of the man he once was. "I have had much time to reconcile the facts with my feelings. They are terrible things, you know?

Facts, I mean. No matter how much you hate the things, they never change. No matter the rage you feel in your heart, there is nothing that will stop them from existing. Maria had much to do with that." He mentioned his wife with affection. "She is visiting family in Corpus Christi. She left an hour before your plane landed, though she wanted to see you."

Wiping away a stray tear, I took a sip of water. "I didn't want any of it to happen, Don Salvador. I tried getting out of the weirdness. It pulled me right back in, and took her away."

"You knew she was with child?"

My heart gave a shuddering lurch. I nearly dropped the glass. "Not until just before the end."

The Don sat back in his chair. "Then the ones who did this crime are doubly damned. I am sorry, my son."

"She said I was the detective, and I needed to figure it out." I let out a bitter laugh. "Some detective. I don't figure it out until after it doesn't matter anymore."

"Why did you come here, Thomas?"

"I had to ask your forgiveness, sir," I said simply. "Failing that, I would accept your punishment."

For the first time, the Don laughed. "You have done nothing to be punished for, *mijo*. It wasn't your fault, nor will I allow anyone to say it was. I told her to return when she got your message. If there is to be any blame, then I must share it.

"The question is," he continued, "what will you do now?"

"I go after the bastards who set it up."

Renton spoke up from the bar, a glass of amber liquid in his hand. "Tom believes the cultists were not the masterminds, that someone else was directing them."

"What proof do you have?"

"Something the old man said, about being neither the potter's clay nor the potter, but the potter's tools." I drained the glass, the water filling me with new strength. "They were bankrolled by someone with a lot of juice, in this world and the others."

"What do you need from me?" Don Salvador's face was earnest as he pulled his phone from his shirt pocket.

"You believe him?" Renton sounded doubtful.

"Mr. Renton, that is my son-in-law. He believes there is something more to this, then I trust his judgement."

The Don's words filled me with hope, something I hadn't felt in so long, it was nearly an alien emotion in my chest. "The cultists were traced to a tribe down in the Yucatan. No one knows how they got in-country."

"I will find out."

"There was a stone altar along with them. Huge thing." My mind pulled the details Mac gave me. "Weighed about as much as a bus but was the size of a Volkswagon. That can't have been easy to get into the country."

"You're right. It cannot have. It will not take long to find."

"Thank you, Don Salvador."

"When you find those responsible, what will you do?"

I paused for a moment, my index finger tapping on the glass. "One of us won't be walking away."

The Don nodded. "I have kept my promise to my daughter, to become more the man she can be proud to call her father. I think, this one time, she will grant me an exception."

In that moment, Don Salvador and I were of one mind, wishing to give the target of our vengeance their just desserts. There was no doubt in my mind I would kill the ones responsible. It would be the first time I ever killed for pleasure; I hoped it would be the only time.

"Don Salvador," Renton said, his glass untouched on a coaster on the bar, "your man said he would come back in five minutes."

"Yes?" The older man wrinkled his brow.

"And to bring you a snack."

"I did, yes. You speak Spanish?" The Don shook his head. "Of course you do."

"The five minutes was up four minutes ago."

"My men are not bound by the clock as you are. Guillermo will return."

That was when, of course, the lights went out.

"I don't think he will, Don Salvador." Renton had a Glock pistol in his right hand.

"How many?" My senses were in overdrive.

"Down!" Renton flung himself at the floor while I tackled the Don back in his chair, sending us both sprawling in relative safety behind the furniture. I chanced a look up.

Bullets burst through the wood, sending splinters everywhere. The doors shuddered under the assault, but didn't break. There was another burst which made several more jagged holes and blew off the top hinge on the left door. No light shone from outside the study, making the fireplace the only source of illumination.

"We have your attention, yes?" The voice was mocking, drifting in from outside the study on a wave of sarcasm.

"How many?" I mouthed to Renton, who held up five twice, then four. Fourteen. Crap. "You could have just made an appointment at my office!" My voice boomed in the enclosed room.

"We've been waiting for you, Keeper. You come out now, we just kill you. The old man and the agent, we give them a five minute head start."

To the Don, I whispered, "You have a panic room in here."

He nodded. "I do. How did you know?"

"You're way too smart to be stuck in a room with no exits. Where?"

The Don crawled to a nearby bookcase and pulled out a hardcover copy of Papillon. I nearly laughed at the joke. There was a small click, which gave way to a door opening. The Don pulled it open, revealing a dimly lit room filled with the comforts of life. "We can stay here until help arrives."

"You can, sir. They're here because of me. The least I can do is take care of the problem for you."

"You have the count of five before we come in there and just kill all of you without a thought, Keeper!" The voice was maddening. It had the sound of familiarity, but it was completely one-sided. They knew me, and knew me well. I didn't like that feeling at all.

"Okay! I'll come out!" I looked over to Renton, who had produced another weapon, this one hauntingly familiar. "Just a minute. You got me; what's another minute?"

There was a muted but heated conversation near the right door, then, "Fine, you got your minute. Make your peace with whichever god you think will touch your worthless soul."

"Get in there and stay in there, sir," I whispered to the Don. "I doubt anyone can get in there if you don't want them to. I won't have your death on my conscience too. Please."

My plea was answered, and the Don entered his panic room without another word. I secured the entrance and moved the book back to its rightful place. By my count, I had thirty seconds or less to come up with a brilliant plan. Unfortunately, I had nothing except a stupid plan. Oh well: you go to war with the plan you have, not the plan you wish you had.

I got Renton's attention and pointed at the bottom of the door, then held up three fingers. He shook his head, held up four fingers, then nodded his head to the right. I smiled in spite of myself and nodded in agreement.

"Your time is almost up, Keeper. Make this easy!" That wheedling voice was enough to give me the mental shits.

It also gave me a target. "I'm coming out!" I took off at a dead run, four steps before I leaped into the air and screamed "Now!"

Renton's Glock spat a single bullet, striking the hinge exactly in the right place. It hit a fraction of a second before my feet hit the door flat. The bullet tore through the metal, allowing my mass to finish the job of tearing the door out of the frame. Both door and detective flew through before crashing into two enemies who were standing in the path. As amplified as my senses were, I felt and heard the crunch of a skull crushing under the weight of wood and my body. The other fell to the side, grabbing at his face, a huge splinter sticking out of his eye, screams coming out of his mouth while blood and pus filled it.

More bullets whizzed by me, so I twisted the door in mid-air to my right and kicked, sending me in one direction and forty pounds of solid wood the other. I felt the wake of the bullets passing like hornets chasing me, pulling at my shirt collar and pants legs.

I landed unceremoniously on my stomach to the sound of multiple weapons trying to fire on empty magazines. My mind screamed at me to get up and run, but I couldn't leave Renton and the Don. I scrambled to my feet and prepared to face my death.

"Your death will be swifter than you deserve, murderer," one of the gunmen spat, the magazine from his military-issue assault rifle dropping to the hardwood floor.

I saw Renton from the door, holding a gun in his left hand. "Tom!" He tossed it toward me before falling back under a hail of fire.

Without thinking, I lunged forward, grabbing whatever he threw at me, wanting to catch it and use it, whatever it was. If I had to die, I would go out on my feet.

My hand wrapped around the checkerboard grips, worn from many hours on the range. The tritium sights on the black steel were just bright enough to see in the dim, and the metal housing of the gun itself seemed to swallow the light. It greeted my hand like an old friend, which it was. I didn't bother looking to see if a round was chambered; Renton would have already seen to that.

My thumb flipped down the safety on the Beretta, bringing it alive, bringing me alive, and bringing death to every son of a bitch I could find.

"Oh shit," one of the other gunmen muttered. "Shoot him!"

As the cold fury fell across my mind, a smile formed across my face while my gun hand came up. If I was capable of speech at that moment, I could have said only two words. They would be the last two words the men in that hallway would ever hear.

Too late.

Chapter Seven

Breathe. Aim. Slack. Squeeze.

That was the standard formula for any shooter, whether with a rifle, a shotgun, a handgun. Whatever the weapon, the way to make sure to hit whatever is in sight is to follow that mantra. It's a simple four-step way to ensure, if not a kill, then a hit, which is really all anyone can ask for.

In a firefight, multiple life-threatening conditions come together into single life-saving decisions in instants. The crisscross of light wars with the harsh shadow, trying to play tricks on the eyes and make you miss. An errant breeze can push the barrel off by just enough to wing the target instead of kill. The loud crashes of gunpowder going off in an enclosed room slamming the eardrums with enough force to nearly bring tears to the eyes.

That was what the formula was for: to make all those factors almost non-existent, and to keep the shooter from losing their cool when the bullets start to fly. It's a nice thought. Poetic, even. It possibly even saves lives every once in a while. Hell, maybe it gave the silly bastard who came up with it the warm fuzzies.

Of course, in a real firefight, breathing takes too godsdamned long.

Time slowed down for me, letting me see everything as it happened. I ducked down and to my right just as my trigger finger squeezed, the bullet impacting my target's forehead. A burst from the assault rifle flew over my falling form, gouging out the floor, the splinters bouncing off my pants. His head snapped back, a gout of brain and bone exiting the skull and painting the man behind him.

I took my first breath.

I swung around on my heels, crouched, my ears barely picking up the squeaking of my sneakers on the hardwood floor. My gun was aiming on its own, picking out two more targets. They weren't people, men, or even human. They were targets, little better than the pieces of paper I put thousands of rounds through over the years. The pistol bucked in my hand twice, and two perfect circles appeared in their heads, their unloaded rifles clattering to the ground.

Four down and ten remained. I allowed myself to fall onto my back to get out of the way of a quick three-round burst, bullets like deadly insects flying over my chest. My breath didn't leave me when I struck the floor, allowing me to aim up and to my left, where the burst had come from. My own shot struck right where I wanted it: under the chin, traveling up at about twelve hundred feet per second. Muscle and bone posed no hindrance to the projectile, sending a fountain of brain matter out of the skull.

I rolled twice to my right and kicked one of nearby miniature tables at an assailant. The thing sent a solid shock through my legs as it flew into the man's knees. I heard the screams begin when the legs bent the wrong way and he fell to the floor, the bones sticking out through flesh. I twisted onto my stomach and launched myself at the wailing man. My left fist caught him solidly between the eyes, sending him back to the floor gurgling. I threw myself to the side, trying to keep whoever had a weapon guessing.

Second breath, and my gun spoke again, three loud barks. My shots were slightly lower this time, the bullets hitting the throat. This had the added benefit of severing the spine, cutting the life from three men like a chainsaw on marionette strings. I leaped for one of the dead men as he began to fall. My left hand grabbed the military black ops-style vest and pulled the corpse on top of me as three of the remaining killers managed to reload their rifles. The high-powered rifle bullets hit my meat-shield, making the corpse dance in fits and jerks. Three more shots from my pistol ended their lives with no fuss or fanfare, leaving the remaining three armed men now diving for cover.

On my third breath, I threw the dead weight to my right and jumped to my left. When two stood up to fire, I beat them to the punch, my bullets exiting their left temples, and their eyeballs pushing out of their sockets from the passage of my shots. They dropped like stones, and only twitched in the last reflexes of life.

Time returned to its normal speed, as did my breathing. My heartrate was a steady sixty beats per minute, and I wasn't winded at all. I felt the holes in my clothing from near-hits; I would worry about those later. The caul of emotional sterility fell away slowly, bringing me back to the world and leaving the uncaring side waiting for the next time. I knew it wouldn't be long.

I stood in front of an overturned table, knowing the last one was crouched behind it. His breathing was loud, even over the ringing in my ears from the gunfight. There was no doubt I had the drop on him, and could end his life with no more thought than I would a cockroach. My left hand squeezed into a tight fist, the tendons in my arms aching, while my right clutched the Beretta, the grips digging into my hand, reminding me what I held, what I had done, and what I still had to do.

"Come out." The two words fell from my lips like stones. I raised my gun again. By my mental count, I had two bullets left. "I won't ask again."

"I can still kill you, Keeper," the voice behind the table said, the words betraying the bravery by quivering. "I can shoot you through this table!"

"Good point." I fired twice into the table where I heard the voice. There was a cry of pain, muffled by gurgling. I walked around the table to survey my handiwork, my gun open on an empty magazine. My first bullet had caught him in the left lung, the second in his right lung. I knew the air rushing out was being replaced by blood, drowning him with every faltering breath. He was dying on the very stuff that flowed through his veins, and the look in his eyes, now that I could see them, told me this guy, this killer, was nothing more than a tool, just like the cultists, and just like them, he was useless.

As he died in front of me, I squatted to get close to him. I pulled out his sidearm, still in its holster, and checked the ammunition. The bullets fit my gun, but not the magazine. It didn't matter; the model I had could be loaded from the top as well as the mag. Slow, but when you didn't have a spare magazine or time to load one, it could be a lifesaver. I racked the slide on his weapon, ejecting a 9mm cartridge into my hand. That went into my own gun, and I closed the slide and put on the safety.

From nearby, I heard a moan of pain, then another groan, but from farther away. I recognized both, and unsheathed a knife from one of the nearby dead men. Standing up showed the aftermath of the gunfight, and it made my stomach roil.

There were bodies and blood everywhere, the red stuff leaking from the heads and throats of the corpses. Shell casings were littered on the floor, with blood pooling in the bullet holes in the hard wood. I saw gouges everywhere in the walls, even in the dim light, the damage extensive. Glass had broken during the fight, and I didn't even hear it. It crunched under my shoes as I walked the few feet to the only surviving killer, who was reaching ineffectually for his fallen rifle.

Had he been capable of standing, the man would have been over six feet tall. His chest was broad, and he was hitching in breath to try and keep alive. His blue eyes were wide with pain in the balaclava he wore. White bone stuck out of his clothing with jagged ends, a result of the table breaking his kneecaps and him dropping directly on his thighbones. They apparently shattered and the bottom halves were what I was seeing. Even then, he kept reaching for his gun, gloved fingers pulling him ever so slowly, ever so painfully, towards it. I heard the scraping of bone on the wood, the sound like nails on a chalkboard.

I kicked the rifle out of reach completely and looked down on the poor bastard. The face was covered, but I could see the sheer hate in his eyes, the blue burning like the hottest part of the flame. I felt the hatred, even if I had no real idea what it was about. Usually, when someone hates me, I have a good idea as to why. Time to get some answers.

"Who sent you?" My words had some heat to them, my rage beginning to run again.

"One day, Keeper, one of us will get you." The answer was muddled, but coherent.

"Spoken like a true fanatic." I crouched down, the knife out and under his chin. The point was nestled just the place the throat meets the underside of the chin. "We can do this the easy way or the fun way. Tell me, and I'll shoot you in the head, make it quick or jerk me around. See what happens. The choice is yours, and the clock is running."

Rusty laughter came from behind the mask. "You'll never learn, Keeper, not until it's too late."

"How do you know to call me that?" I pushed the point of the knife, one of those wicked-sharp and functional-looking types, up. The point disappeared a small fraction of an inch into his flesh, bringing a hiss of pain. "Tell me!"

"My payment is your pain, Keeper."

The cryptic answers were beyond pissing me off. "Last chance, Chuckles. You want it quick and painless, or long, drawn-out, and hurtful?"

His eyes cleared for a moment, then I saw the outline of a smile under the balaclava. "There's always another way, Keeper." With that, he grabbed my hand and shoved the knife at an angle up through his skull.

As I said, it was a sharp, functional knife, and the point was honed to perfection. The blade severed his tongue at the root, sliced clean through the spine, and exited out the back of the skull. There was a spasm from the new corpse, then nothing.

Gods, what the hell kind of sick fucks were after me?

I let the body fall and walked back to Renton, who was picking at his chest, where there was a hole in his suit jacket. "You okay?" It seemed like a dumb question, but considering the guy looked like he had taken a bullet, it also seemed a safe question.

"I learned my lesson last time from being around you," the agent said, his voice betraying his pain only slightly. He pulled out a flattened piece of metal and let it fall to the floor. "The latest in body armor."

"Nifty." I opened up the panic room, barely dodging a thrown knife. It sailed past my ear, whistling as it stuck itself in the ceiling. "We got it taken care of, sir."

The Don emerged, a small but very business-like pistol in his left hand. Only he would lead with a knife. "I was wondering when you would open the door."

"It was a near thing," I said, collecting my thoughts. Behind me, Renton was calling for a cleanup crew. Damnation, that man was efficient.

The reality of the situation finally set in. "This is an outrage! They dare attack me in my own home!" He put away the pistol and pulled out his phone again.

"I was their target, Don Salvador. You were an unfortunate innocent bystander in this."

With a toothy grin, the Don said, "They are about to see how innocent I am." A button was pushed and he began talking in rapid-fire Spanish.

I went to Renton, who just finished his own call. "Crew is on their way, Tom."

"Good," I answered. I wondered what the Don's wife would say if she saw the aftermath of slaughter in the next room. "The Don's pissed."

"And rightly so." Renton lowered his voice. "He's on the phone with the governor. None of it is complementary."

I grimaced. Someone was getting a reaming, and would likely lose only their job if they were extremely lucky. That brought up a question, which I asked Renton.

"We had to file a flight plan, and coordinate with local and federal law enforcement. Three hours is enough time to pull together a team for something like this, but they would have to either be right on our backs…"

"Or have someone on the inside," I completed. "Just can't trust anybody these days, eh?" I shook my head and put my gun at the small of my back. "How long until the crew gets here?"

"Twenty minutes. This is a bit out of the way for anyone." Renton tapped a message into his phone.

"What are you doing?"

"Letting your mother know you're safe." Before I could say anything, Renton continued. "She would know a cleaning crew was called, and where it was going. Do you really want her to hunt either of us down before she knows what's going on?"

I backed off, mainly because he was right. I started trying to think of how anyone could get a team of trained killers through the Don's security so easily. Three hours isn't a lot of time to pull off an operation like this. Even though it failed, it came perilously close to working, and all I had to show for it was a bunch of corpses, a shitload of bullet casings, and one really creepy dying declaration.

The Don hung up and looked at me. "This was not how I pictured our reunion, Thomas."

That surprised a laugh out of me. "No, I pictured more talking, less bullets flying everywhere." I hooked a thumb at Renton, who was on the phone again. "There's a crew coming to clean this up. They're very good, and they'll definitely make sure your wife won't easily know something's happened."

"You have my thanks, my son. As for the other matter, I will forward you any information I get." The Don's eyes narrowed in anger. "They have made a grave error."

"That they have, sir. They went after my family again." I smiled, though this time without humor.

"This will not end well for them, Thomas."

I nodded in agreement. "No, Don Salvador, but I assure you: It will end."

The rage, almost forgotten in the back of my mind, roared. It would no longer allow itself to be denied. I shushed it with a single thought, a single promise. Soon, it would be released.

Gods help whatever was in its way.

Chapter Eight

We spent the night in a local No-Tell Motel that might have been brand new around the time Santayana first came on the scene. It wasn't terrible, but any place that wasn't riddled by bullets and bodies was pretty okay with me. I wasn't even sure if we were in an actual town, as deserted as the place was around the hotel. All I knew was we were somewhere between Brownsville and our next destination. I told Mac someone owed me a solid, and whether the guy who owed me knew it or not, I was about to collect.

It would be at least another four hours before we got where we were going, and we were taking our time. Driving made a bit more sense than flying, since we would have more maneuvering options on the ground in case more armed psychos decided to come after us. I wanted to arrive by dusk, since that would allow more of a crowd-shield, as whoever was after me seemed to want to keep a low profile.

Not so with the gods who were pulled down by whatever I did in that warehouse two years before. The television, a babblebox of epically stupid proportions, droned on about these strange beings with the intensity of paparazzi over the latest antics of a celebrity. Flipping through the channels, I found no fewer than eight reality shows featuring various deities, one cooking show starring Bacchus, and a dating game hosted by none other than Astarte, a Canaanite goddess of sex and love. I lingered on that last show, mostly in disbelief.

"It's not as bad as it seems," Renton said, coming out of the bathroom. Whatever the hotel's other failings, there was nothing wrong with the hot water.

"They're enjoying this." My words were dripping with surprise. "They actually like being brought down here."

"Don't think that for a minute." The agent was in his boxers and a wifebeater, a towel over his left shoulder. "All they're doing is adapting to survive. They aren't as powerful as they once were."

I turned off the television, disgusted at the sight. So much for regality and staying above the mortal fray. "Lovely. So you're telling me they're like the Superfriends on Ecstasy?"

Renton chuckled at that. "Yes, but some of them are more like the Legion of Doom on crack. They pretty much police themselves, though, which is good news for us mere mortals."

"Right. I know how well they take care of things." My stomach burned with acid from the memories of manipulation.

"Go shower. You need it worse than I did." He handed me my Beretta. "Just in case."

I left the room as the agent put on his suit like a ritual. Thanks to the cleaning crew, who had replaced his clothing as well. I had no idea how the guy could wear a suit in the heat, but it apparently worked for him and saved his life. I guessed it was as much a part of him as it was his eyes or hair or hands.

The gun went on the sink and I put a towel over it, just to keep it from getting wet. Steam filled the small room immediately, the shower running hot. I stripped down and got under the water, letting the stream move my mind back in time.

The Don had been pleased by the speed and care shown by the agents assigned to fix up his mansion after the firefight. We spent a couple of hours strategizing over what we, meaning Renton and I, were going to do after we left Brownsville. To say the Don was upset about the attack would be like saying skinny-dipping in napalm might result in a slight burning sensation.

"I will skin them alive." The Don's words rang with the finality of an executioner's axe.

"Can't say I blame you, and we're working on that," I assured Don Salvador. Renton was conferring with one of the agents on the scene. I couldn't tell who it was, but he was nodding to whatever was said to him. "We're heading out after the crew leaves to pick up the trail."

"You have a lead?" Renton asked.

"More like an informant who might know exactly what we need. They'll talk, or things won't go as well as they did for the bastards here."

Don Salvador seemed mollified. "Very well then, my son. Make them pay, not only for the death of my daughter and your wife, but for the murder of my men here." The Don's voice hardened. "They worked for me but they were family all the same."

I nodded in understanding. "Then your loss is my loss, and it won't go unanswered."

A smile graced the Don's lips. "You are a good man, Thomas. You understand the value of family. My Susana chose well."

I answered with my own sad smile. "She will always be the one, Don Salvador. Always and forever, it will be her."

Renton chose that moment to interrupt. "Excuse me, but the crew is finished. It should be just about perfect, but the crew will be happy to return for any reason." To the Don, he said, "There will be four teams on site for security until you say otherwise, sir."

"They are trained?" The former crimelord raised an aristocratic eyebrow. When Renton nodded, the Don asked, "By you?"

"Initially, and completed by her." The agent didn't have to clarify who the "her" was.

"Then I am in the safest of hands."

"Don Salvador, this is my fault," I began. "I'm so very sorry."

The Don held up a hand to stop my words. "Enough! You had nothing to do with this, my son. I do not hold you responsible for the attack, or the destruction it caused." He leaned forward in his chair and pulled me close, his hand on my neck, until our foreheads touched. "No apologies. No sorrow." His words carried venom, directed not at me but to whoever had decided to make themselves our mutual enemies. "Your only responsibility is to make those *putos* pay in blood. You understand?" His eyes were bloodshot with unshed tears, red-rimmed and brimming with barely concealed rage.

"I do, Don Salvador." My own voice was raspy, my rage choking off each word.

"Then, when it is done, you let that pain go." The Don's tired smile returned. "Don't let it finish the job of killing you that those *cabròns* started." He squeezed the back of my neck with strong fingers. "I say this not as her father, but yours. This world needs you alive and in the present, not dead and in the past. Promise me, in a way I know you will keep."

I swallowed and let my eyes close.

"I promise, on the love we both have for Susana, Papa." I had never called the man Papa before, but it felt appropriate and right.

"That is all I ask." The Don released me, strength returning to his voice. "Go. Finish this."

My eyes opened both in memory and in life. The water from the shower was still hot, but my skin didn't feel it. My hands were on the sweating wall, propping me up under the stream. I felt the tension burning out of my shoulders and neck, though I could still feel where the Don had placed his hand. I hadn't told him the obvious, that I might not survive the coming battle, nor the not as obvious: that I almost didn't want to. I imagine he would have hit me upside the head a few times to get me straightened out, or told me in that kind steel voice that I would keep going no matter what happened.

I switched off the water and inhaled the steam, letting it clear my head. There was the steady drip of the water in the tub as I stood still, the humidity in the small room condensing on me. Though my hair wasn't as long as it once was, it still caught enough water to make rain when I ran my hand through it. With a deep breath, I got a towel and dried off, letting ideas go in my head as they would.

Someone knew we were in Texas. More to the point, someone knew I was back in the world, and in the weirdness. That implied connections on both sides of the veil, which scared the hell out of me. Something like that would mean I didn't have some little punk hopped up on a temporary power pellet like Pac-Man after me. Working both sides was something a major power would have to either be involved with or would have to do themselves.

The towel wrapped around my waist, I began shaving, as the scars on my face would not allow for an even beard growth. The supplies were store-brand generics, which worked for me. While the blade sliced through a couple days' growth and some runny shaving cream, I realized the whole plot went deeper than that. Whoever was responsible for what happened at the warehouse was likely the cause of everything, going back to the beginning. It made some sense, actually. The godslayer, Raziel, the coins, all of it had to come from a common source, someone who wanted to set this whole thing in motion. I had a few ideas on that front, but I needed to make certain a couple of things.

Hence the favor I was collecting.

When I came out of the bathroom, Renton already had my clothes laid out, with a light jacket that looked loose enough to hide the shoulder holster for my Beretta. I dressed silently as he took our few suitcases out to the new Honda we appropriated under one of his aliases. The holster had a familiar feel to it, which made sense as it was my old one. Slowly, things in my life were coming back together. As I slid the weapon into the well-weathered holster, I felt another piece of me return. The jacket was an almost-perfect fit as I picked up my own bag and met Renton out at the car.

"Are you sure you're ready for this?" Renton's voice had a touch of worry.

"It has to be done." My voice sounded more firm than my resolve. "He owes me big, and this is the best lead."

Renton shrugged and got in the Honda. I took shotgun and checked my phone. No messages, which was not that good. It meant Rika had nothing yet, making my hunt more difficult. It also meant Mac had nothing, either. Of course, it had only been a day, so I shouldn't have been expecting miracles.

We drove in silence for several miles before I decided to check my other source. "Larry."

The spirit responded instantly, appearing in the backseat. He was dressed in a cream-colored suit, perfect for the beach about twenty miles to the south. Larry seemed much more at ease than he was the last time I saw him. "Yes, Thomas?"

"Anything about that Achilles thing?"

"The Order of Achilles is not a 'thing', Thomas." The spirit seemingly had regained some of his peevishness, which I took for a good sign. "In the last two years, it has gained a membership of thousands in well over a dozen countries. Those inducted seem to have forgotten that Achilles had to be tragically deceived into helping take Troy, and he did it out of vengeance, not duty."

I caught the rebuke under the rebuke and let it go. "Fine. What did you find out about the Order of Achilles?"

"Better." Larry crossed his legs, getting comfortable. "After a bit of digging, I managed to discover that while the Order was founded in Athens, Greece, its main office on this side of the world is located in none other than Chesapeake, Virginia."

"That is pretty weird," I commented.

"Not at all. The Fall started in our area, our 'neck of the woods', so to speak, and for the most part, that is where the gods and the like landed." Larry straightened his cuffs and tilted his head toward me. "There were exceptions, of course, and one of them was Achilles. He started his order in the wake of the 'gods craze' which followed their arrival. I have to say, mortals do love jumping on bandwagons. First those insipid celebrities and now gods, demigods, and their spawn. It would be disheartening if it were not so humorous."

Renton cleared his throat and said, "Social commentary aside, Larry?" I still wasn't used to other people being able to see Larry.

"Of course. Essentially, one had to be of great bravery and martial skill to be a member."

"Pettiford must have slipped through the cracks to get in," Renton said. "He had very little in the way of bravery when we saw him."

"Do not be so sure. He was a war veteran, and decorated for bravery and valor."

I butted in. "How do you know that?"

"I went to the Order's home and asked." Larry gave me a superior smile. "I do speak ancient Greek, Thomas."

"Fine, but that doesn't explain why he was missing his heart, or why all those other people had been killed there."

"On the contrary, it explains several things, as a great many of those murdered there were members of various societies of a warlike nature."

"Artemis?" I asked. "Ares?"

"Among others." Larry uncrossed his legs and leaned forward intently. "What it comes down to, Thomas, is they were all possessed of great valor and bravery and they were murdered in the same way. It also seemed to happen the same day of the week, every week for two years."

"Which day?" I already knew the answer.

Larry went somber. "Need you ask?"

"No, but I figured I might as well." Sunday. The day she died and the day I vanished. I turned to face the front of the car. "A sacrifice. A weekly sacrifice."

"For what purpose, I have not the foggiest idea." Larry sounded distraught.

"They were trying to make sure the gods stayed here." My voice was flat like a dead man's heart monitor. "Because they couldn't cut my heart out, they used others as proxies, to keep the gods powered down and on this plane of existence as much as possible."

"That would speak of planning the likes I have never seen, Thomas. It would require people in every place, looking for the perfect victim, then bringing them to that cursed place, and then cleaning up before your mother's people found anything." Larry sounded impressed.

As well he should; something like that was incredibly difficult to keep going. Unless they were fanatics, and considering what I was exposed to already, that wasn't out of the question, they would have to make a mistake eventually. My mom would have found something out eventually. The question was, why did they stop being so godsdamned careful?

The miles rolled underneath us in silence after I sent Larry to find some more information about the murders themselves. I considered a few possibilities before the obvious answer hit me between the eyes. The only reason to not stay out of sight, to not be careful, was because you didn't need to anymore. I was back, and they could end me easily, to make sure the big hoodoo they put on the gods was permanent, or worse, made them as weak as mortals.

The why was becoming clear, as was the how, but the who was still fuzzy. Whoever did this had a serious hard-on for the gods and, for some reason, me. Whether the hating of me was because of my connection to the gods or something personal I had no idea. However, considering the way they got to the gods was through me, the damage done to me and my family had the feeling of being an unexpected bonus.

I broke the silence as we crossed the state border. "I'm unfinished business."

"What's that?" Renton had kept quiet during the exchange between me and Larry.

"Why stay out of sight any longer? They kill me, they get what they want, and they don't have to keep doing it by proxy anymore." I laughed, bitterness coloring the mirth. "I'm the godsdamned brass ring."

"Which makes this little trip even more dangerous," Renton cautioned. "If they want you dead and don't care anymore, a crowd won't keep you safe."

I shook my head. "No, they're not going to be that blatant yet. They want to have me handled before they go for primetime. I'm a loose end that's just aching to be tied up. They act too soon, they get everybody after them."

"They already have a police chief, a crimelord, and the head of a spy agency after them," Renton muttered. "Isn't that enough?"

"Not when you consider these bastards have been planning this likely since long before Gilgamesh ruled Ur." I tapped my fingers on my leg, nervous energy showing in the gesture. "This had start so long ago, and so subtly not even the gods would know about it."

"And it all depends on killing you? I wish I could believe it's that simple, especially when you're making it seem that complex."

"I'm part of it, probably a big part of it. Susana, too." The more I thought about it, the more it made sense. "Each time something happened, I was always reacting, moving in the way they probably wanted."

Renton cleared his throat. "You might want to invest in a tinfoil hat, Tom." He held up a hand to forestall the retort I was about to make. "I'm not saying you're completely wrong, but no one, even the gods, can predict everything. After all, they didn't see the Fall coming." I had to give him that. "I think you're a large part of the plan, but plenty of room for error. No one can plan for every eventuality."

"Okay, but explain how the Fall happened if it wasn't a grandiose plan to bring the gods down."

"I'm not saying it wasn't." We passed a sign showing under three hours to our destination. "What I am saying is don't try to make things more complicated than they need to be. Yes, you are likely a loose end, and someone is trying to take care of you. It is entirely possible you're as important as you think. However, no plan survives contact with real life. That's something we both know quite well."

The hell of it was, Renton was probably right. I let the conversation idle as we made our way east, the setting sun at our backs. Yeah, I was pretty important as a go-between the gods and mortals, but with the Fall I became even more important, since I was pretty much the only one who could really understand and reason with them, if you called what they did "reasoning". Take me out of the equation, there was no one who could work as a liaison. Then it hit me.

Kill me, and there was no more Keeper.

That was the pleasant thought crashing through my mind as we made the outskirts of what was one of my favorite cities and, personal tragedies not included, a place of wonderful memories. Renton smiled as he slowed to the speed limit. "Welcome back to the Big Easy, Tom. You know where we're going?"

I checked the time. It was just after ten in the evening, which was good enough for me. My phone said the place was open until "the last sunrise", which meant it never closed. That fit the proprietor to a tee. He liked that sort of thing.

"Yeah, I know where we're going." I started giving directions to the French Quarter. When we got within a mile,

I told Renton to park; there was no way we could get through the streets by car without going full Grand Theft Auto. Once we were on foot, I set a quick pace for our destination: Mouri Man Pati.

The Dead Man's Party.

Not surprisingly, the line to get in stretched for nearly a quarter-mile, and I had no doubt every single person would stand in line until Judgement Day to get inside. The Mouri occupied not one, but three storefronts, which considering the price of retail space on Bourbon Street was astounding. I had no doubt the proprietor had worked some magic to get such a deal.

I mean actual magic, as in voodoo.

The windows looked like they had neon designs chasing each other, until I realized there were actual glowing creatures going after each other in the windows. They were likely coerced spirits, even more likely former patrons of the Mouri who traded service to the loa for some stupid reason. The front was covered in ironwood, which was again no surprise. With the amount of energy inside and out of the club, there would need to be exceptionally strong building materials involved. I had no doubt other measures were taken to make sure the place wouldn't suffer from a slight case of explosions. When we got closer, I saw the charms hanging from the rafters, little human-shaped fetishes covered in hair and other body items, and the protective symbols carved into the wood. There were mostly the faux-disaffected youth in line, waiting with studied impatient nonchalance to get into the club where all was permissible.

I barely gave any in line a moment's thought as I walked past the bouncer, who promptly put a hand the size of a pizza pan to my chest to stop me. He towered over me by a full head and was half again as wide. The suit he wore was loose in deference to the humidity. I didn't see a weapon, but then the guy could have been carrying a bazooka and I would still go in like a godsdamned boss.

Polite as you please, I said, "I'm going to see the Baron."

"I'm sorry, sir, but you'll have to wait in line, and the Baron isn't in tonight." The smile was plastic, the manners wooden. Gods, the whole place was a fabrication.

"I think you misheard me," I answered, a smile on my face, as genuine as his. "I'm going to see the Baron."

"I don't think---" was as far as he got before Renton did some really cool trick involving the knuckles of his left hand and the bouncer's left trapezius muscle. It was like a Vulcan death grip that actually worked. A choked cry of pain came out before he apparently passed out from the pain.

"No," Renton said, "you don't." To the next people in line, he smiled, that dangerous smile he saved for when the blood was up. "Don't come in quite yet. Keep an eye on him.

Thank you." The mascaraed men held up their hands in surrender and fear.

"Thanks," I said, pushing through the swinging door.

"No problem," Renton answered. "You know we're not going to be welcome here for long."

My eyes swept the undulating ocean of people, the multicolored lights flashing of sweaty flesh, music beginning to pound my ears. I could vaguely see the band at the far end over the heads of three hundred people, and I was suitably impressed. The bass line was strong, and when the Lady doing the vocals began to sing, I had to let out a laugh.

"Is that…?" Renton trailed off.

"Lady Miss Kier," I shouted. "Come on, Renton. Haven't you heard that groove is in the heart?" For the record, I love that song.

We pushed our way past knots of people standing together, some dancing, some swaying, and nearly all under the influence of some kind of narcotic. The Baron was known for loving intoxicating things, and this was just more of the same. Alcohol and absinthe, wormwood and hashish, they all mixed together to create a perfect place for letting the mind and soul free.

My eyes kept looking for some kind of sign of the Baron, but instead, at the bar, I spied someone I knew all too well. Red began to tinge my vision, and it wasn't the light show. My mouth began to work, opening and closing. No words, just movement. My feet carried me at near a run, slipping around people like smoke as I made my way to the bar. In only a few short strides, I made it, shouldering aside a pair of painted people who might have just been figments of someone else's imagination.

Facing away from me, the bartender's head was shining in the light, with sweat glistening off it. He was a slight man, not more than five and a half feet tall, weighing a buck-fifty at most. There were scars on the top and back of his head, but I had seen him in profile, the spectacles perched on his nose a clear giveaway. He was skinnier around the middle since the last time I saw him, but there was no mistaking the pinched features of the former Doctor Paul Luvec.

The coroner-turned-bartender turned to face me, cleaning a glass with a pristine white towel. "What will it be, sir?" he said, not looking at me.

"What's up, Doc?" I shouted during a second's lull in the music.

Luvec's face shot up and he screamed "You!" before I grabbed him by the shirt and pulled him over the bar. My fist started pummeling down on his face, pounding the flesh and bone into new shapes and colors. I snarled and batted away his hands as he tried to protect himself. Each hit sent a jolt up my arm as I kept hitting him, shattering his nose and sending his glasses into the crowd, which formed a semi-circle around us.

I just hit him, over and over again. Blood was on my knuckles, from the shot that turned his nose into a bleeding tomato. It dripped onto his face with every punch. I sat astride Luvec's chest, pounding my fists into his face, Hard, methodical punches, designed to hurt and destroy.

My mind was numb. This was one of the links in the chain, but I didn't care. He was one of the ones who took part in the destruction of my life. That I cared about. He was part of the plot that ended up killing Susana.

That I definitely cared about.

After what seemed like an eternity, I punched him one more time, letting his head bounce against the hard floor. Standing up, I let him curl into a ball and nurse his wounds. The whimpering was loud and, to my surprise, audible. I realized belatedly the band had stopped, the people were quiet, and everyone, even Renton, was standing aghast at the savagery of the beating Luvec received. My hands ached, but that didn't matter to me. I wasn't done with him yet.

That was, until someone said I was.

"Now Keeper!" The boisterous voice cut through the silence with laser-like speed. "Why you breakin my property?"

I turned to face the Baron. "Good evening, Baron Samedi." You're looking well."

The nearly nude black man, top hat at a jaunty angle, loincloth not covering everything, was leaning on the bar. He held his head in one hand and a cane in the other. "You not answer me, Keeper, and the rules not what they used to be. You tell me why you breakin my property, or I have my boys tear you to pieces." Not the way I wanted the audience to start, but at least I had his attention.

Yay me.

Chapter Nine

The last time I was in New Orleans, I stopped an insane coroner with delusions of genocidal grandeur from turning everyone in the world into the walking dead. I also rescued the loa known as Baron Samedi, the voodoo master of life and death, from captivity. There was even a wedding in there somewhere, if memory serves. Coming to the Big Easy always ended up being a life-changing trip.

So there I was, face to face with a nearly-naked and visibly pissed Baron Samedi, a broken and bleeding former-genocidal-coroner-turned-bartender at my feet, and a crowd of restless club goers arrayed around me. The Baron looked ready to breathe flame, his knuckles grey from tightly gripping his cane. Luvec, the little bastard, was still curled up and weeping, covering his bleeding and broken face with his hands. Some of that blood was still on my fists. Renton stood at the edge of the crowd, his suit jacket open, his right hand clenching and relaxing, ready for anything but eyeing me warily. He had never seen me cause so much damage with my bare hands. Neither had I, but there's always a first time for everything. The faces in the crowd looked at me with a mixture of awe and fear, and I liked it.

Nice to see I still know how to make an entrance.

The Baron stood and approached me, his bare feet padding on the wooden floor, the cane tapping in time to his steps. Up close, he looked a lot like I remembered him: strong, muscular, and just powerful. I could feel the energy coming off him in waves, but I stood against it. I would not cower in front of him. That invited attack, which contrary to popular belief was not what I wanted.

"I be waitin, Keeper." Baron Samedi smiled a toothy grin, and I could smell the bourbon on his breath with each word, hitting me with a cloud of alcoholic haze. "You damage my prop'ty. I need to damage you?"

"He'll heal," I said, my voice level. I truthfully had no sympathy for Luvec. He had caused so much pain and anguish that what I did and still wanted to do to him was sweetness compared to the monstrous things he caused.

"Oh yeah, he heal, but it take time. He belong to me." The Baron tapped the groaning form on the floor with his cane none too gently. That brought a louder whimper. "Long as I am, he live. Death not take him til I'm good and done wit him."

"He's got something I need, Baron."

"That not my problem," the Baron responded dismissively. He lifted the cane and tapped my chest with the jeweled head. "You my problem, Keeper."

I sighed. "Is that right?"

"Dat exactly right. You bring us all down like we answer to you. You make this mess with de Conclave. Dis ain't how it supposed to be." Each sentence was punctuated with a poke in the chest. "You cause a lot of pain."

"Yeah, I know about pain, and I know this motherfucker," I kicked Luvec lightly, causing a weak groan, "caused enough of it to deserve what I'm going to do to him."

"He not yours." The words were delivered flatly, though I heard the implied menace under the tone.

"I don't want to keep him. I just want some information."

"It his choice to give it to you."

Gods, the Baron was playing games with me. "You owe me." I said the words low enough for only him to hear, catching and holding his gaze like a cobra does a mongoose.

There was a pause, then, "You can't keep him."

"I don't want to keep him. I want fifteen minutes with him."

That raised a shaggy eyebrow. "And then?"

I smiled. "And then he's yours and I don't give a shit what you do with him."

"And then?"

It took me a second, but I caught his meaning. "And then we're square."

That brought a wide grin to the Baron's face, and a roar of laughter. "That what I want to hear!"

I reached down to grab Luvec's blue silk shirt, the blood drying to look like chocolate milk stains. "He can't die, right?"

"Not until I let him, and that be a long time."

"Good." I nodded to Renton, who bent and got a handful of Luvec's shirt along with me. "We'll take this outside. No need to get the floors dirty."

The Baron flapped his hand at us, showing his dismissal. "Fifteen minutes start now. Don' be late."

Renton and I bundled Luvec out of the club, past the gawkers and staff and through the doors, leading with the good doctor's head first. Once we were back in the humid air of the French Quarter, I pulled Luvec from Renton and slammed him into the wall. Wood and metal rattled along with glass from the impact. Renton watched from a few feet away.

"Hey, Paulie, remember me?" I brought an elbow around into the side of his head. Remarkably, he wasn't bleeding as much as he was, and his nose had almost gone back to normal. Flipping him to face the wall and shoving him nose-first into the wood fixed that, with blood exploding from his abused nostrils. I flipped him back to look at me. "Remember?"

The undying man gasped in pain and nodded his head jerkily. Fear oozed from his every pore, and that was exactly what I wanted.

"Who gave you the mojo?" I asked, punching him in the stomach as hard as I could. Luvec gagged and tried to double over, but I would not let him. "Someone gave you that mojo bag, you stupid bastard. Who?"

There was a moment of defiance, a flare from the eye that wasn't completely closed from abuse. "You can't kill me, Keeper," Luvec smiled, broken teeth showing from behind his lips. "I can't die."

"True, but I can certainly make the next few minutes very bad for you." I pulled Luvec close, the scent of the cinnamon mints he chewed on his breath. "There is a level of pain that will buy you, and not everything will grow back." I sent a knee into his crotch, which had the desired effect. "I can make things happen in the space of a minute that even the Baron will have a tough time coming back from," I pulled Luvec away from the wall and slammed his head against the hood of a nearby car, "and I still have more than ten minutes with your sorry ass."

Luvec slumped to the dirty concrete when I threw him back against the wall. The overhead lights shone on his pate, and turned the blood almost black. I sent a foot into his gut and barely dodged the results of him emptying his stomach. Another kick, and there were dry heaves.

I squatted down next to Luvec. "Think I can't keep this up? I can do this all night. Fifteen minutes is just the warm-up." I smacked him across the face, as he appeared to be trying to fall unconscious. "Not yet, Poindexter." I gripped his forehead in my hands and squeezed. "Understand this: I will give up everything I have to the Baron if I need be to get what I want." A hard push, and Luvec's head bounced off the wall and into my fist. "There is no way this is going to end well for you."

"Tom?" Renton sounded odd, but I just chalked that up to seeing the new me for the first time.

"Not now," I said, never taking my eyes off Luvec. To the bartender I smiled. "Where did you get the mojo?"

"Conference!" Luvec screamed in my face. I backhanded him, more to keep him focused than anything else.

"What conference?"

Luvec said nothing for the moment, but a good shake got his tongue wagging. "Some police conference years ago." Luvec spit out the blood in his mouth, the mixture of blood and teeth sickening. "I got approached, like I was known down there."

I pulled him to his feet. "Who?"

"Some guy. Seemed really important."

"Name?"

"I can't tell you his name."

That brought the fury right back, and I pounded on him for a solid thirty seconds, mostly in the stomach. I didn't want to damage his mouth. When the punches subsided, I slammed him against the wall again. "In case you couldn't tell, that was the wrong answer. Who?"

"I don't remember!" Luvec wailed. "There were so many people there, I can't remember who it was. He was really important, though. He was in his dress uniform and everything."

"What about the nametag?"

"Tom?" Renton said again, his voice uncertain.

"Not fucking now, Renton," I spat from the side of my mouth. "Come on, Paulie. You're doing so well. Tell me what I want to know and you can go back to your weird eternal indentured servitude." I pulled out my gun. "Don't, and I'll make sure your mind is on everyone." I smiled. "It won't kill you, but I doubt you'll enjoy pulling yourself together again, and I will make sure every second of it hurts."

"It was a long name, I think," Luvec muttered. "It's hard to remember."

"You were a coroner and considered top of your field around here, you sick son of a bitch." My gun connected with the side of his head, the sights causing a cut. "You lived for details, and you remember this one. Now talk!" I pushed the barrel of the Beretta into the center of his forehead.

"Okay! I remember! Just don't hurt me anymore!" Luvec screamed, tears of pain and anguish running down his face.

"Who." I pulled the gun away and stepped back, ready to get back to hurting him if I had to.

"I met him at the police conference for violent crime. It was in some shitty convention center. He gave me the mojo bag, the Baron's bag." Luvec started crying more. "I didn't know what it was at first, but then he gave me a book to learn how to bring back my family. Said I could do more with it than that. He said I could beat death."

"Yeah, by killing everyone else and yourself at the end. I've heard this part already, Paulie." I reached forward and rapped him on the top of his head with my gun. "Bored!" I rapped him again, this time in the forehead. "You're also an idiot for buying it."

Luvec sniffled. "He was a cop."

"And? I'm getting bored again."

This time Luvec closed his eyes and seemed to really concentrate. "I'm thinking! He seemed really very nice. Respectful, even."

"Get slobbery on him later, Paulie. Who was it?"

"Give me a second!" Another moment, and Luvec's eyes opened up wide, his gaze bright. "I remember!"

Which was, of course, when his head exploded.

I heard the three gunshots from above and behind me, which did nothing for my well-being. Those bullets could have easily found the back of my head. Whoever was shooting wanted the good doctor to shut his trap, and three rifle bullets did the trick.

There were strong hands grabbing my shirt and pulling me behind a nearby car, which also brought Luvec with us since I still had a death grip on his shirt. The twitching of the body was unnerving, since it was missing a face and part of the top of his head. I couldn't put it down to a death twitch, since it was entirely likely Luvec really was still alive. His hands started moving of their own accord while his feet kicked at the ground in obvious pain. I released the man and readied my weapon.

"That's what I was trying to tell you, Tom," Renton said, his gun already out. "The street is empty."

There was a barrage from above and to the right, the bullets hitting the roof of our cover. That was the opposite direction as the shots that took down Luvec. Another burst from above, this time from straight ahead. I chanced a look over our cover, and I pulled my head back very quickly. Three teams of snipers above at a range of less than a hundred feet? That wasn't an ambush.

It was a slaughter.

From our left and right came shouting, though not panicked shouting. These were the crisp clear commands of a military operation, calling out positions and numbers. I looked up and down the street to get an idea of how screwed we were. At the sight of two four-man teams in full black-ops gear each direction, I shut my eyes in frustration. We'd gone from porn star to IRS audit recipient.

"Renton, we have a problem." I took the extra magazine out from my holster and held it in my left hand.

"Tell me about it." Renton remained stoic, even with several bursts fired in his direction. Sparks flew from the ricochets.

"They've got us pretty covered."

"Yes." He turned to smile at me. "They have us right where we want them."

I narrowed my eyes and picked out where the bullets were coming from. It was pretty easy to do so, since the answer was "everywhere." "What are you going to do?"

"Just be ready."

Centering myself took an instant, and I gave Renton a nod. "Okay."

"Hit what I miss."

Renton reached down, grabbed Luvec by the front of his shirt and stood, putting the body in front of him. Bullets smacked into what should have been a corpse. The agent sprinted around the car, keeping the body between him and the barrage. His gun came up and fired six times in rapid succession, the boom of the Desert Eagle rebounding off the storefronts in a way the rifles did not.

I moved to where Renton had just been and looked above. The son of a bitch had given me clear shots at the snipers, and I took them. My own gun, though not as massive as Renton's, was enough for the job, six bullets finding the skulls or eye sockets of the snipers and their spotters. That made life a little easier, though we still had at least a dozen trained killers after us.

Then I looked over at Renton.

The street was narrow, with cars here and there on both sides. It was empty as far as I could see, with only small sandwich boards tented out on the sidewalk. Renton used Luvec as a shield just long enough to get close to one of the fallen soldiers laying in the middle of the street, then tossed the body at one of the teams hiding behind a truck. The motion took their aim off him just long enough for the agent to pick up one of the submachine guns in his now free hand. He somehow twisted around in almost a ballet pirouette, bringing the SMG to bear on two soldiers out in the open. Renton opened up with the weapon, spraying bullets into their bodies. They danced for the last time and fell to the hard ground.

With the magazine dry, Renton threw the weapon, tucked and rolled, picking up another submachine gun. Still on the ground, he turned over and fired, keeping the barrel steady. The stream of lead went under the truck, striking the enemy in the feet and legs. They fell screaming, right into the path of bullets that struck them elsewhere, uniformly fatally.

Renton rolled again, this time to his feet and behind the truck he had just made safe. He threw the SMG to the side, letting it clatter in the street. I didn't get to see what he was doing much longer as the two teams of killers decided at that moment to come after me. Bullets struck my cover, the car rocking from the hits. I couldn't even stick my hand out with just my gun because of the amount of fire coming my way.

I saw Renton crouch-walk against the truck, to within where I thought I saw another car before I had ducked down. As the killers paused to reload, I heard one of them shout a strangled "Hey!" That brought me up enough to look over the front bumper of the car.

The man I knew only as Mister Renton was in the middle of eight trained killers. Renton had his left arm wrapped around the throat of one of them while spraying the remainder with one of their own weapons. Three soldiers went down, blood pouring from the holes in their bodies. The new human shield struggled until he took a burst from an enemy, bringing Renton's attention on the killer. The SMG was empty, so Renton threw it at one of his targets. He dropped his shield but grabbed a knife from the corpse's belt as it fell. With the dexterity a card shark would envy, Renton threw the knife, embedding it to the hilt in the third from last soldier's throat.

The second to last killer was trying to clear a jam from his weapon as Renton walked up to him and calmly, with almost a sorrow, grabbed the guy's gun and pulled him close. Renton's gun barrel was in the bastard's chest when the agent pulled the trigger, and Renton let the guy go past him and fall to the ground with no further thought.

That left one final killer, who seemed to think better of his situation and tried to run. Renton would have none of that, shooting out both knees with a pair of bullets. The guy had gotten only a couple of steps before Renton had stopped him instantly. The agent walked with a purpose to the man on the ground, who was scrabbling to move out of the way. Raising his gun, Renton pulled the trigger again, the bullet going into the back of the killer's head. Its duty done, Renton put the gun back under his coat, which didn't have a speck of anything on it.

He called out one word, surrounded by the bodies of men who were trying to kill us. "Clear."

Godsdammit, that badass motherfucker was magnificent.

I stood up and looked at the destruction around him, and barely believing what I was seeing. He had gone up against a hit team with no cover and pretty much thrown himself against them, getting away without a scratch. It was cold, methodical, and without a doubt one of the most amazing displays of badassitude I had ever seen in my life.

Renton wasn't even breathing heavily as I approached him. All I could think to say to him was "Thanks."

"Part of the job." Renton scanned up and down the street, his gun hand still empty. "I should have seen it earlier."

"We were busy," I said. "Where'd you learn to do all that? I mean, I'm good when I have the element of surprise, but you just went full Rambo on these guys."

That brought a sheepish smile. "I learned from the best."

He meant Mom, of course. "Another cleaning crew, I take it?"

Renton nodded. "This is getting to be a bad habit." He nodded his head towards the bullet-ridden yet still moving body belonging to Paul Luvec. "Too bad we didn't get what we needed."

I shrugged. "We got enough. I have an idea already, but I want to make sure. That means we're going."

"De fawk is dis?"

I spun around at the indignant voice and saw the Baron Samedi had decided to come on out to see about all the hubbub. He went to Luvec and ran his hands over the torn and bleeding body. It was strange seeing the Baron so gentle, especially with someone he considered his property.

"I'm sorry about that, Baron," I said, not really feeling sorry at all. "Someone popped him while he was talking. Not our fault."

The Baron didn't seem very convinced. In fact, he looked righteously pissed. I couldn't really blame him, but I wasn't the one who put a few dozen holes in Luvec. "Dis not like you, Keeper! You use to care about people! What happen to you?"

"Nothing time won't fix, just like your property, right?" I put my own gun away and turned to leave. "We're even, Baron. Sorry about the mess."

As Renton and I walked away, I heard the Baron wheeze out "Da *mess*?" and had to bite back a laugh. I knew it was the aftereffects of the adrenaline rush that made me want to laugh my ass off. I had all I needed from Luvec, which, while not a lot, was a hell of a lot more than I had before I arrived. I wasn't expecting to get much, and maybe I went overboard with working him over, but I had to make sure. I had to know.

As Renton made his call from the driver's seat, I went over the clues in my head. There was a cop out there who was behind everything done to me for the past several years. Someone who had made it their mission in life to manipulate mine. Each time I had a case, something was off about it. Granted, something was off about all my cases by their very nature. That didn't mean there wasn't something in the background, something that just didn't gel right with me and the way every event seemed to push me down a path destined for that horrid day.

It did mean, however, that someone I knew was calling the shots on my life. Not only that, but they had set me up to bring down the gods to nearly mortal level, and had done it without anyone knowing. That spoke of some either phenomenal luck or exquisite planning. I'm talking a mix between Batman and Doctor Who-levels of planning, and even then it wouldn't work. These were the gods. They had power levels that started at nigh-omnipotent and went up from there. Setting something in motion like the Fall was impossible. The gods made mortals. It was like your big toe planning to take over the rest of your body; it just doesn't work. It made no sense.

So I sat there, trying to figure out who hated me that much, and how they could pull off the greatest coup ever of all time. No one fit the bill. Not even close. It was frustrating, and I was spinning my wheels. When Renton said the airport would have the jet ready by the time we got there, I just nodded. There was something I was missing, and I was starting to get the feeling I was running out of time. Two kill squads in as many days? That's a sign that someone didn't like me.

That meant I was getting closer.

Chapter Ten

The trip back to Norfolk was quiet and thankfully not uncomfortable. Renton was on the phone nearly the entire way while I crashed hard. Sleep was always a long time in coming for me, so an unexpected nap always did well for me. Granted, the adrenaline burned out of my system was the likely culprit, but I wasn't about to look a gift horse in the mouth.

We touched down a bit after midnight, and I was groggy all the way back to the office. I was never a morning person, and for me, morning was just after I woke up, no matter what time it was. Renton handled everything, and in the time it took to get out of the airport parking lot, I was conked out again. I woke up just long enough to get into my office, grunt a thanks at Renton and a hello at Larry, before tumbling into my bed, out cold.

Morning came too quickly, as it always did. Sunlight slanted through the window, which burned right into my eyes. I was still in my clothes from the night before, the t-shirt wrinkled, the pants askew on my waist, my shoes not even off my feet. I was a mess, at least clothes-wise, but I couldn't have cared less, as I doubted the President was going to stop by anytime that day. Kicking off my shoes, I began my morning ritual, working out the frustrations of the two prior days in sweating repetition. By the time I was done, my clothes reeked and were unfit to wear.

I took a quick shower and dressed, trying to get my bearings on the day. With all that was going on, it seemed things were coming to a head. I was closing in on the great mastermind behind all the terrible things that happened, and I knew I would have revenge on the one who set it all up. What needed to happen, though, was I needed to make sure nothing altered the plan.

That meant I had to do some terrible things. Huzzah.

When I was clean and dressed for the day, I walked out of my room into my main office. Renton wasn't there; he must have gotten the message. My computer was running already, the fan humming quietly in the early morning stillness of the room. I moved the mouse just enough to wake up the monitor. My breath left me; the pain in my chest was like an electric shock flowing through my lungs I broke down in tears.

The picture on the screen was from a few years ago, my brother-in-law's birthday. The whole family was there: mom, my brother-in-law, my sister, my niece and nephew. They were all arrayed around me and Susana, with her showing off her lack of skills at dancing. The camera had caught me catching her. What looked like a dip was me keeping her from breaking her head on the floor. Her hair was flowing like an ebony waterfall, her mouth open with a devil-may-give-a-fuck laugh. It was the last big family gathering before winter, and I could see her ring, a simple band of silver around her finger. It caught the light, shining like a beacon, drawing my eye to it and wrenching my heart from my chest.

The storm quieted after a few minutes, and I centered myself. Pulling up the email on my computer blocked the picture, making it easier for me to focus. I wiped away the tears and read through a few items, all the while waiting for the terrible things I had to do. It wouldn't be easy, but it had to be done. I only hoped for forgiveness, and a chance at redemption.

I snorted at the word. Redemption. We always hurt the ones we love the most, and sometimes, there wasn't any going back.

My first business of the day was to contact an old friend, and someone who was instrumental in my plan. A quick email went out, simply saying "Text me when you're here." Approximately three seconds passed before an abbreviated version of *La Marseillaise* began to play on my phone. I should have known he wouldn't be far.

"Come on in, Luc," I called out, loud enough for anyone indoors or out to hear.

The door opened and Luc Bertrand entered in a subdued manner, quite unlike the man I knew years before. He was not an imposing man; far from it. Luc was an average height and build, and wore loose-fitting clothing to further disguise his body. He wore an ivory hoodie, with the hood up and covering his head and obscuring his face. Though it was cold enough for ice outside, his breath didn't plume in smoke. I would have loved to know how that trick worked. Once the door was closed, he pushed back the hood, revealing a face older than last I saw, the cares and worries of a man ten times his age etched upon it. It made some sense; after all, he was the head of the Order of Assassins on the East Coast. That would put pressure on anyone.

I smiled as he approached my desk, his hands in his pockets. That was both a good and bad sign. Good, because it meant he felt the office was safe. Bad, because he had a lot on mind and his plate. A thought flitted through my mind if someone had ever come to him for a contract on my life. I figured whoever asked wouldn't be long for the world, but I had to wonder what would be offered.

Pushing down the speculation of how much my death was worth, I stood and offered Luc my hand. "It's good to see you again, Luc."

The Frenchman looked at my hand as if it were some kind of alien artifact. Slowly, with difficulty, he pulled his hand from his pocket and took mine. There was warmth there, hesitant, but friendly warmth. "Just as it is good to see you, Thomas." He released my hand and sat at the chair I gestured. "You look well."

"Don't believe everything you see, man," I smiled again, trying to get past my friend's moodiness. "I learned that lesson the hard way."

"As have I," Luc grunted.

Well, it didn't seem there would be any real banter. Time to get to business. "I suppose you're wondering why I asked you here."

"I have an idea."

That caught me flat-footed. "You do?"

"You want my life for not stopping the bad information getting to you." Luc raised an eyebrow. "Am I wrong?"

"In a word," I said, "you are very godsdamned wrong. I know you wouldn't have set us up, not knowingly, and that little girl who faked being one of your people is somewhere on my to-do list---"

"And mine, I assure you," Luc interrupted.

"Just so. However, she can wait. I have bigger fish to fry." I took a deep breath. "And I need to do it alone."

Luc seemed about to agree until he comprehended the last thing I said. "*Quoi? Qu'est-ce que tu dis?*" Catching himself, he repeated himself in English. "What are you saying?"

"I'm saying, Luc, that I'm not going to need your help on this. Just stay out of the way." I put a little more steel into my voice. "This doesn't concern your order, or you. I can't have anyone else get hurt on my account."

"This makes no sense, Thomas. If anything, you need my help. This is more than you can handle alone."

"Be that as it may, I don't need you." I stood up and moved to Luc's side of the desk. I put my hands in my pockets as I leaned against the desk. "I know you've got more important things going on than a grudge match between me and the guy who put me away for a couple of years."

Luc stood to face me. "*Au contraire*, I have spent every moment since your disappearance trying to find the *fils de salop*. I cannot allow you to face it alone. Honor demands it."

I shook my head sadly. "Not this time. I ask you this as a friend: don't help me. Don't get involved. This is my battle, and it is one I have to fight alone."

Luc closed his eyes and inhaled sharply. "You are certain?"

"If I could have it any other way, I would." A sad smile crossed my face. "I'm sure."

My friend, the assassin, put his hands on my shoulders and pulled me to embrace him. "Then I wish you more luck than your enemy, and should you fall, I will be there to avenge you."

I pulled my hands out of my pockets and returned the hug, going through the motions of getting a kiss on each cheek. I never could get used to that gesture. "Thanks, Luc."

He pulled away, eyeing me warily. "I understand. *Bonne chance, mon ami.* I hope your meeting with the two ladies goes well." Luc headed for the door, opening it and gestured for Rika Elder to enter, followed by my mom, Avaline Statford. With a Gallic chivalry that brought a smile to both ladies faces, he held the door open, exiting after they came in.

My mom stopped a bit behind Rika, a touch shorter than the cop. Avaline Statford was an older woman, with silver streaking through the reddish-blonde of her hair. She kept it tied back in a simple ponytail, as she preferred function over form. That was also evidenced by her choice of clothing, which was jeans, snowboots and a parka, the latter of which likely covered anything from a switchblade to a sniper rifle broken down for easy assembly, or anything in between. I wouldn't put anything past my mom, as she was the head of a spy agency so secret it didn't exist. I learned a lot from her, and the most important lesson was to make the hard decisions and live with them.

She also taught me I would probably never like those decisions.

Rika tossed her coat on the chair Luc recently vacated. "So what did Monsieur Frenchie want?" She said mocking the French accent.

I leaned against the desk again, my hands in my pockets up to the wrist. "What did you find?"

Rika seemed a bit put off that I wasn't answering her, but she let it slide with visible deep breath. "Well, okay. From the information Renton sent over, there were a few suspects. All of them are current police commissioners and chiefs of various forces across the country." She pulled out a notepad, something of an anachronism, and began to scan through her notes. "I've looked through everything I can find and no one fits the M.O. Are you sure this guy said it was a cop?"

"That's what he said between beatings," I said, "and I'm inclined to believe him."

"Then it's not a local cop." Rika shrugged. "I have a couple of leads through INTERPOL thanks to your mom, but I just don't know."

"Hi, Ma." I gave a hint of a smile.

"Hello, Tommy," she answered, her voice soft. My knees went a bit watery; it wouldn't surprise me that she knew what I was thinking. It was her job to read minds. "How are you feeling?"

"I'm okay, Ma." It wasn't completely untrue. I learned the best way to lie was to tell just enough of the truth to satisfy the listener. Ironically, I learned it from her. "I'm glad you both are here. We need to talk."

Rika whipped around and looked at Mom in confusion. "About what?" Rika asked.

I took a deep breath and blurted it out. "Your services are no longer required."

"Huh? The Fuck? What?" Rika's mouth dropped open, and I saw her eyes flash dangerously.

"This isn't your fight anymore, Rika, and it really never was." I didn't let her recover before diving in. "I just needed information, and you got it for me. Thanks. Now, I need you to let it go and go home." I gripped the chair with her coat on it. "That will be all. Thank you."

"What in the blue hell?" Rika's voice rose in volume, becoming a roar. "Who the fuck do you think you are?" Her neck began to crane and her hands rolled into fists.

My words were stone to her fire. "I'm the guy who lost his wife and his world. You've had time to get over it. I haven't, and this is how I'm going to do it: by my self." Before she could get another word out, I said, "That is all."

In the time I knew Rika Elder, I had never seen her at a loss for words. Sure, I had seen her shocked, even dumbstruck, but there was usually some kind of statement she made as it happened. The Memphis in her wouldn't allow her not to say anything. It wasn't just in her DNA; it was in her very soul.

That was why the way her mouth worked, opening and closing, in pure surprise made me almost break and laugh. It was the most terrible and amazing thing I had seen in a long time. I just hated I was the cause of it.

Before she could discover what words were, I cut her off again; I picked up her coat and tossed it to her. "Bye, Felicia," I sneered, to finally get the point across.

Apparently, I did. She screamed in unbridled fury and frustration and grabbed her coat out of the air. The fury was from the dismissal of my words, the frustration was from not being able to twist my head from my shoulders due to my mom being right there. Rika flung the door open so hard, the doorknob left a dent in the inside wall.

As the door closed, I knew I had hurt her, and hurt her badly. We both knew what the phrase "Bye, Felicia" meant. It was a double-edged saw blade through her heart. It was the last thing her ex-fiancee said to her, in the same dismissive tone. He had been drunk, and likely didn't know who he had just dismissed, and even more likely didn't care. The guy was a total bastard, cheating on her with everyone else just weeks before their wedding. It had taken everything I had to keep her from killing him right then and there.

And there I was, reopening an old wound, and dousing it with salt and lighter fluid. Some godsdamned friend I was. I closed my eyes and massaged the bridge of my nose with my right hand, while my left hand went back into my pocket.

"That was cruel." Mom's words fell flat on my ears, no emotion coloring them. "Needlessly cruel."

I shook my head. "No, Mom. It was necessary." I lowered my head down so I wouldn't have to look at her.

"I am disappointed."

Those three words cut me deeper than anything in life. "I know."

"I have never seen you do or say anything like that to anyone who called you a friend." She approached me and tilted my chin up, so my eyes would meet hers. I saw the judgement in them, and it was not at all favorable to me. "Had she decided to knock you on your ass, I would not only have let her, I would have helped her. What happened to you while you were gone?"

"I learned that I have to be cruel to be kind."

"I taught you better than that."

"Yes, you did, and I've always trusted you." I put my hand over hers. "This time, I need you to trust me. I need you to know that I know what I'm doing. Believe it or not, I do."

Comprehension dawned in my mother's face. "You know who did it."

"Yeah." I smiled, the expression feeling alien on my face. "I put it together from something Rika said. It's so damned obvious." I squeezed her hand tightly. "I need you to let me do this my way."

My mother, the woman who had taught me everything I knew, from which fork went with which dish, to how to field strip a heavy machinegun, let two tears slip, one from each eye. There were others that wanted to be shed, but she kept the crying at bay through force of will. "You're going out there to die."

"Probably."

"Will it be worth it?"

"Probably." I let a grin form. "I'll try and make sure he dies first, if that's any consolation."

"It's not, Tommy." She put her arms around me and held me close. Her face went into my shoulder, and I felt the unshed tears there. I put both my arms around her and I almost felt my control slip. Almost felt my iron melt into cotton candy. Almost just threw the whole idea out the window and wanted to curl up in my mommy's arms and let the world burn.

I couldn't do it. The lady who birthed me, the lady who held me when I was young, and held me on the eve of my potential destruction, didn't raise me to give up. For better or worse, I was committed, and there was no turning back. "I'm sorry, Ma. I have to."

"I understand."

With that, she turned on her heel and walked out, more quietly than Rika, but the closing of my office door held enough finality that I felt a cold hand grasp around me. Was it the feeling of my coming revenge? I couldn't have said. All I knew was I had just either sent off or pissed off everyone I knew and cared about and who cares about me. Just as I had been two years before, I was facing off with an enemy without anyone at my side. Only this time, it was by my own hand, and it was nobody's fault but mine.

Chapter Eleven

It was all so simple; I couldn't believe I didn't see it before. In fact, I mentally kicked myself repeatedly on the cab ride to my destination. It was like one of those optical illusions that are only obvious when it's an inch from your face. Until then, it was nothing more than a jumbled mess that made absolutely no sense. I didn't see the pattern until it was entirely too late.

The cab was dirty, dingy, and reeked of what I hoped was just urine, even though there was a lower, muskier odor beneath the sour tang. I didn't have any other transportation, as Renton was no longer available, and I completely understood why. I counted myself lucky he wasn't present at my office when I had it out with Rika. Otherwise, I would have been scraping my spleen out of the ceiling with a spatula if I was lucky. As it was, I had already burned every bridge I had ever built.

All of them, save one.

As the cab negotiated traffic down Jefferson Avenue, I mused on how strange my life became after becoming the Keeper of the Conclave. So many beings called me both friend and enemy, some of them in the same breath. So many times I risked dismemberment, death, and worse, trying to help these gods, it became a nearly-unbreakable habit. Other times, I protected mortals from the clutches of the gods, or the lesser types of critters out there. Sometimes I won, sometimes I didn't. There were so many amazing sights I witnessed, things my mind treasured and turned over in such agonizing detail. The Bifrost in all its glory, the rainbow bridge to Asgard and all points in between. An group of archangels enjoying a cookout on a summer's day, their perfect features split by huge grins. Inanna allowing me to watch the dawn with her in the Fertile Crescent, where no other mortal ever set foot. So many wonderful and wondrous things, and all because I was chosen to bear the mantle of Keeper.

I looked up as the cabbie came to a stop, exactly where I told him. His grubby hand was out, so I tossed him a couple of large bills and exited the cab as quickly as possible. The door slammed behind me with more force than I meant, but it was worth the baleful glare of the cab driver as I took a deep breath of relatively clear air. Newport News never smelt so good. I stood there a moment and took stock of things as the cab peeled off, likely hitting forty from a dead stop.

The t-shirt was one of my favorites, a grey one with the Batman symbol emblazoned across the chest. It was tucked into a pair of black jeans, so new the crease was still sharp enough to shave peach fuzz. The belt was simple leather, the buckle hammered silver. My coat was the long leather duster Susana bought me after I professed a love for the Old West garment. Even though the last time I wore it was before she died, the black leather was still supple from the layers of oil that were worked into it. With the gusts of frigid wind, the coat billowed out behind me, becoming almost a wing of shadow. The hair I grew back in the time since my return was thicker, but the breeze still bit into the areas of unprotected scalp. There was no doubt I was an imposing figure, even with my black Chuck Taylor hightops on my feet.

I put my hands in my coat pockets and pulled the leather close to me, trying to keep some warmth. That I chose this place to make my stand was no accident. It was a lot like fate, even if those old biddies who called themselves the Fates wouldn't admit to it. Mortals make their own fate; that was what fascinated the gods so much with us. Sure, for the most part, the odds were rarely in anyone's favor to go against the grain, but every so often, there were one or two who broke all the conventions, defied all the odds, and thumbed their noses at the universe and her gods.

I knew I was one of those. A spoiler. A monkey with a wrench. A fly in the ointment. A complete pain in the ass. I tried getting out of it, but it seemed that when your whole existence is to laugh at normalcy, things have a way of pulling you right back in. It would have been funny if it weren't so damned inconvenient. Of course, what was I?

Right then, I was freezing my ass off on the side of the road near the Newport News International Airport, where I was not a day before. I waited until around nightfall to make the trip, making sure I arrived when the sun was completely down, and dark had taken over. The road was just as long and just as uninviting as it always was, a chill that had nothing to do with the temperature, invaded my bones. I took several deep breaths, plumes of steam coming out of my mouth before stepping off the paved road and onto dark earth.

Even after years of staying away, the woods by the airport had not lost their fearsome visage. A wall of pitch-black started not ten feet past the road, and I could see the broken concrete disappear into the lack of light. The path was a mix of stone and overgrown grass gone wild, but it was like a knife cut off everything in existence past that certain point. Light seemed to just vanish, and I knew something was waiting for me in there, and it was hungry.

I was in there once many years before, when Mac was a simple police lieutenant and I was just getting into the private eye gig. I even died in there, if only for a few seconds. Lester Gibson was found in there, dressed in a mockery of Zeus's attire, electrocuted to death, then slowly cooked from the outside in. A horrible and sick way to end someone's life, but it was surprisingly the least crazy thing to happen that night.

My feet stopped at the edge of the dark, and I felt the caress of something along my left leg, urging me to take one more step. Just one more little pace into the Dark, where I wouldn't worry about anything anymore. A place where being nothing was the norm, and it would feel good to just give up and go into the black. I knew that feeling quite well; it had been part of me while in Niflheim, piecing my broken mind back together.

There was an almost audible wail when I turned my back on the darkness, both from behind me and in my head. That part of me, the one that wanted oblivion, cried out once and was silent again forever. I would not go gently into that good night, and I sure as hell wasn't going to give up. I whispered my friend's name.

"Thomas," Larry said as he appeared. He wore a purple silk shirt, open at the throat, and similar-colored pants. The look in his eyes spoke not of fear; he could have whatever lurked in there for breakfast. His eyes were pictures of concern for me. "Why are you here?"

"This is where I have to be, Larry. Nobody will sneak behind me. " I put a brave smile on my face, the emotion about as genuine as a politician's promise. "Besides, this is where the end begins."

"You know who it is," Larry said. I nodded. "Then it truly is time."

"They've been watching me for a good while now." I indicated with my eyes and chin where the three groups of soldiers were doing a poor job of hiding.

"Indeed. Are you ready for this?"

"I'm ready."

"Must I leave?"

My voice caught in my throat. Larry was my friend, but I had fought my way out of Niflheim without him. Of course, I didn't know I had him as a friend at the time, but it didn't change the fact I had done a great many things without him. This was just one more. Damned if it didn't hurt like a bastard, though.

"Yes, Larry, you must. Go." I took my left hand from my pocket and pointed at him, shouting the word again. "Go! Do my bidding!"

Larry's eyes widened, and in a blink, he was gone.

Which left me alone, as it had to be.

"Okay," I muttered to myself, lowering my hand to my side. "This is the way it has to be."

I pulled my right hand from my pocket, my fist clasped tight around something I had carried since waking up three days before. I opened my hand and smiled, my tears refusing to fall at the sight.

It was a little thing, nothing fancy. No inscription. No whorls and lines and engravings. There were a couple of scratches on it, and I knew exactly where each one came from. It was pure silver, or as pure as I could find. There was a mate to it, smaller and thinner, and as far as I knew, my mom had it. The one in my hand, though, was mine. Men's size eleven, made for thick-fingered galoots like me. I remembered the last time I wore it, and the pain hit me with the force of a punch. Gritting my teeth, I inhaled sharply and held the ring, my wedding ring up to the dim light of the stars.

"For you, babe," I whispered. "Always and forever." I slipped the ring on my left hand, the metal warm from my touch. It felt exactly as it should, and with that final piece of me, I was as whole as I would ever be, and ready to bring about an end to the bastard who started this.

"Oy!" I screamed, looking at the nearest group of soldiers, hiding ineffectively behind a trailer left to rust in a parking lot. "You want me? Your boss want me?" When there was no movement, I stepped away from the darkness. Holding my hands up, the light of the nearest streetlight gleaming off the ring, I shouted, "No more running!" Still nothing. I challenged them again, crossing the road away from the dark hollow. No need for the protection; I knew where they were.

Finally, I grew tired of the whole mess. I had crossed the street and they were still hiding. In frustration, I screamed, "Come and get me, you horsefuckers!"

That seemed to do the trick. A small team of four men advanced on me from across the street, guns drawn. The trailer they had been hiding behind opened up, and two more men came out, also with weapons drawn. Unlike the team, these two didn't have their guns pointed at me. As the team surrounded me, the differences in the two men were apparent. One was tall, the other medium-height. While both had dark hair, the shorter one has his cut very close. The taller one seemed to prefer his hair longer and in a ponytail. The shorter one appeared in charge, so of course I directed my question to the taller one.

"Was the magic word 'horsefuckers'?" I shook my head in disbelief. "You boys really need to work on your secret code words. Oh, did I hit too close to home?"

The shorter one jabbed me in the stomach with his pistol, a small but very efficient Glock. Police-issue, of course. "I'm the one you have to deal with, asshole."

"'Asshole'?" I mocked. "Did you call me that because that's where your head goes on a daily basis, up your boss's ass?"

That earned me a hard punch to the stomach, bending me at the waist. "You have no idea the amount of pain you just bought yourself, Statford!" I doubled over, trying not to gag. Bastard may have been short, but he packed a wallop. "He-Who-Is-Now wants a word with you before he kills you."

I spat a wad of phlegm in front of Stumpy's feet. To Tallboy, I looked up and laughed. "Does he call the shots everywhere?" I leered at Stumpy, who took my meaning instantly and gave one hell of a left hook, bringing stars to my eyes.

"Be careful, Mort," Tallboy said. "He doesn't want him harmed."

Mort licked at a small dab of blood on his knuckle. "Yeah, I know." That was when he punched me again. "He won't be harmed, within reason." To one of the men covering me, Mort ordered me searched. When they came up empty, Mort was astonished. "You're unarmed?"

"Your boss wanted me, Short Stuff." That earned me another gut punch, making me gasp for air.

Mort pulled my head up by the back of my neck. "Oh, he wants you, Statford." His voice, rancid with breath mints, was no more than an inch from my ear. "He's wanted you for a long time.

"Okay, then let's cut the foreplay and get down to it, you horsefucker." I got a backhand for that one, this time from Tallboy.

"Don't call him that." Tallboy stared at me in reproach.

I let a ragged laugh slip out. "What, you're the only horsey-ride he gets, right?" That earned me two soldiers holding my arms and Tallboy hitting me as hard as he could in the gut. They must not have wanted to hurt me; hitting me in the body wouldn't cause too much irreparable harm.

Unfortunately, these assholes wanted to cause reparable harm.

Once Tallboy got his licks in, and Mort snapped a picture of me with his phone, I wasn't feeling so well. I would have a rainbow of bruises across my face and chest, my stomach taking the worst of it. That, of course, depended on whether I lived or not. At the rate I was going, I would be lucky to make it out of the parking lot. With an effort I kept my mouth shut.

Mort tapped Tallboy on the shoulder and showed him the phone. Gazing intently at the device, Tallbody nodded and spun me around. I felt the cold metal rings of handcuffs go around my wrists, tightened against my warm flesh. Before I could say anything else, a black bag went over my head.

"Oh come on, guys," I groaned. "You're gonna kill me anyway, and you go for the cheese?" I shook my head in disgust. "Son, I am disappoint."

There was no answer as I was shoved into a vehicle that sounded like a van. The sliding door and heavy rumbling of the engine were hints that it was a van, anyway. I was pushed none too gently in between two of the soldiers, one of whom kept his gun embedded in my ribs. The van sped off, pushing me back against the seat.

"So, since I don't know where we're going," I said, my voice muffled by the sack, "I just wanted to let each of you know that this is your last night on earth." I paused for effect. "Every single one of you is going to die."

There was a huge hit to the back of my head, catching me unaware. It hurt like a son of a bitch. "Shut your mouth, Statford," Mort snarled. "Only one dying tonight is you."

"You're going to die screaming, Mort," I said, turning my head in the short man's direction. "I promise you that." That earned me another strike, this time with what felt like the butt of a pistol. That hurt more, but made me smile in spite of the pain. The men around me kept silent, whether to evade Mort's wrath or thinking on my pronouncement of their mortality, I couldn't say.

I concentrated on the route, though it was much harder than I thought. Tallboy was jittery, and bounced his leg constantly. His knee was in the back of my seat, so I felt every single bounce. I sighed and focused as best I could, especially on the several bumps in rapid succession we passed over. They were familiar.

A few moments after the bumps, the van stopped abruptly, and the door slid open. The metal on metal sound was jarring to my ears, but the splashing of waves was there also. I could smell the scent of the ocean through the cloth, and see vague lights through the dark bag. Doing a quick mental calculation, I figured out where we were.

"Well, at least you're killing me in style," I laughed, forcing good humor into my words. "Bringing me all the way to Fort Monroe to die at the Chamberlin? I'm touched, ladies. I really am."

One of the soldiers whispered disbelief at my knowing before Tallboy shut him up with a word. Then, to me, he said, "Nice trick, Statford. It still won't save you."

"You're going to find it takes a lot for me to go down. I bet Mort over there is glad you don't say the same."

The sack was pulled from my head and there was Tallboy, right in my face. He wasn't amused by my taunts, and my lack of fear seemed to finally enrage him. "One more word, and I cut out your fucking tongue. He-Who-Is-Now probably won't mind a bit. Now move!" He grabbed my coat and pulled me roughly toward the Chamberlin.

Built in 1927, the Hotel Chamberlin sat right near the beach on Fort Monroe. For decades, it had been a vacation destination for the wealthy and the well-connected. It was designed in that frame of mind, with the stonework and ornamentation reminiscent of the bygone days of FDR, war bonds, and soldiers going off to fight the Nazis. Deals were said to have been brokered in the rooms of its nine floors that likely shaped not only the Hampton Roads area, but, with its location on an Army post and so close to Langley Air Force Base, the military as well. There were rumors that the rich met with high-ranking military officers in the huge area at the very top of the hotel, but nothing came of it. After decades of serving as a home away from home, the old brick building was no longer as glamorous as it once was. Most of the lower floors were supposed to be turned into a retirement community, but something had gone wrong with the zoning, and it stood empty for years.

Mort began shoving me again, this time through the doors and into the lobby of the Chamberlin. Just as I remembered it from half a decade before, it was immaculate, the checkerboard marble floor spotless and gleaming. Light poured from the fixtures, reflecting off the statues and planters, giving everything a healthy mellow glow. The six men didn't allow me much more to look before hustling me into an elevator. I kept my mouth shut and my breathing steady; there would be no second chances.

When we reached the top floor, Tallboy pulled and Mort pushed me out. They each took an arm, with the team of four soldiers arrayed around me, escorting me to this He-Who-Is-Now. It sounded impressive, but I wasn't impressed. More annoyed, to be honest. I knew exactly who I was dealing with.

This would just make killing him that much more deserved.

The attic area was more like a ballroom, with huge vaulted ceilings coming to a peak forty feet above my head. The elevator let us out at the far end of the ballroom, letting me see all the way to the other end. Beams crisscrossed overhead, with lights lining the wood. Almost all of the lights above were off, with only a few lamps on the floor to provide some illumination. A roaring fire was in the fireplace situated at the very end of the ballroom. There was a raised floor in front of a great circular window, easily fifteen feet in diameter and split into multiple sections. Very artistic, aristocratic even and it allowed the moon to shine through, when it wasn't hidden by clouds.

The floor was hardwood, and clicked with the steps of the soldiers. My own shoes squeaked every few steps, just random enough that I didn't seem to be doing it on purpose, even though of course I was. At the other end of the ballroom, a figure stood facing away from me. The midnight blue suit was a severe cut, looking tailor-made for its wearer. His hands were behind his back, clasping each other, the fingers of the left hand twisting a garish ring with a blue stone on the right. Lush brown hair was what I could see, with a small bald spot beginning at the crown of his head.

I was brought to a stop about ten feet from him, but even from a mile away, I would have recognized the officious prick. Even though I figured it out, and even seeing who it was, I could hardly believe it.

"I was hoping we would have this chance to speak, Keeper," he said, his smarmy voice grating against my ears.

"You know who I am, huh?" I snorted. "That makes two of us."

That earned me a gut-punch, with another one delayed only by the raising of my host's hand. "No need for that. He's not going anywhere."

A sneer on my lips twisted my words. "No, and if I have anything to say about it, neither are you, Parkinson."

Chapter Twelve

Everyone has enemies. It was a universal truth, and anyone who said they had no one who would like their head on a ten-foot glowing purple lance was either incredibly naïve, ridiculously clueless, or made it a habit of killing anyone and everyone who looked at them funny. There was an old saying "a man is known by the company he keeps", and by comparison, I believe someone is defined by the enemies they have.

Of course, over the years, a majority of people who wanted my blood were dead or destroyed. A demon utterly annihilated by angels. A pair of Chinese ganglords dead at the hands of a master assassin. A psycho ate a face full of buckshot courtesy of my wife. So many others no longer a concern after so long, I never thought I would need to worry about someone who had never been more than an idle threat. I mean, everyone would worry about the wolf at their throat, not the jackal in the shadows, especially when the wolves just kept on coming. It was just common sense, and no one could be blamed for missing the signs.

That was how I found myself on my knees in front of Harold Parkinson, former police chief for Hampton and Newport News. Surprisingly, he looked much the same the last I saw him, though he wasn't as scrawny as I remembered. His eyes, formerly a muddy brown, were a sharp topaz, which was very jarring. Parkinson was dressed in a tailored suit, and he definitely looked more vital than anyone his age should. I did some quick mental arithmetic and came to an answer of sixty-three. That didn't track with me, as he had no crow's feet, no laugh lines, no wrinkles at all. His hair was lustrous, even with the small bald spot. From my memory, Parkinson's bald spot was a thing of legend.

"Well," Parkinson drawled. "I was wondering when you were going to show up, Statford."

I laughed, earning a smack in the back of the head. "You're gonna lose a hand for that," I said as I looked up at Mort. I turned to face Parkinson. "You're looking well, Hal," I sneered. He hated that nickname, so of course I planned to use it as much as possible. "Who's your tailor, Hal? Did your mommy dress you after a long night on the corner? The hair's a new look, too. I almost can't see where they stapled the pubic hair onto your forehead."

A thin smile formed on Parkinson's lips, a sorry sight that made my guts churn. He dismissed his team of guards with a handwave, keeping only Mort and Tallboy. "Charming as always. It's been a while."

"Apparently not long enough, Hal." I rustled my arms behind my back, trying to get some circulation in my fingers.

"How long have you been planning this little thing?" I chuckled and shook my head in disbelief. "What am I saying? This isn't something you came up with. You had to put your own birthday on a calendar to remember it." I looked up at Tallboy, who glared back with barely concealed disdain. "Seriously, I saw it. He had to put it on there because he couldn't remember it and no one would remind him."

"You do have a way with words, Keeper, though you'll find that Morton and Tucker are beholden to me, as have their forebears, long before you were even born!" Parkinson waved a hand dismissively, smiling bigger when he saw my reaction at him calling me the Keeper. "Oh, I know all about you, Statford. I've been waiting a very long time for this moment."

"I bet you have, you silly twunt." Both Mort and Tucker smacked the back of my head, setting my ears ringing. "Why didn't you do it years ago? Why all the ducking and fucking around?"

Parkinson lowered his voice to a low conspiratorial volume. "That's not the question you want to ask, Statford, and not the question I want answered."

I nodded. "How did I know it was you?"

He grinned, straight white teeth showing in an even line. "You would have made a fine detective one day,

Keeper. A proper detective, had you not been touched by the gods."

"I didn't, actually, not until Rika told me there were no current cops at the level needed to pull off the shenanigans. Whoever was behind it knew how to get a secret flight plan for a government jet. They also had to know about the Don, and work out a kind of arrangement with the local cops to not be suspicious of no alarm signal coming from his place. That was a nice ambush, by the way."

Parkinson inclined his head at the compliment. "Not nice enough. Your friend still lived."

"You're a penis." I braced for the hit, but a raised hand from Parkinson stopped the blow from falling. "New Orleans was another thing. You knew I was going after Luvec. He was the only one who knew your name, or at least what you looked like."

"Dear Paul was a misguided soul," Parkinson commiserated. "A man without a family, and without hope. I gave him that." He sat down on the edge of the stage, still above me, but no longer having to look down so far. "Honestly, I knew you would stop him; the whole thing with Baron Samedi was to buy some time. Things were almost ready, but I needed just a few more months."

"The altar," I muttered. "It didn't come over the Mexican border, did it?"

That got Parkinson laughing, a braying that grated my eardrums. "Of course not! It came hidden in a shipment of cars landing in the Newport News Marine Terminal. The altar was simple to get past customs, as were the other little tools needed for your part in the drama." He laid a finger against his nose. "Always good to know where the bodies are buried, isn't it?"

"And your cultists came from somewhere else."

He looked confused for a moment, then brightened. "Oh, the 'Tools of the Gods'? Those fools." Parkinson leaned forward on his knees and shook his head. "They'd been waiting centuries for the chance to bring about their own version of the end of the world. I just told them what to do and like little tin soldiers, they did it."

Having Parkinson so close to me was hell; in spite of his dapper exterior, his breath made a sewer rat sandwich appetizing. I gagged and pulled my face back. "Shit, man, if you look in my coat, there's a whole pack of breath mints. Enjoy with my compliments."

Parkinson pulled back suddenly, glancing up at his two men. "You see the abuse I get from this one?" He sighed, but kept his distance.

"So now my question: How do I know what you are?"

"That thought had crossed my mind."

"I've known who you were for years. I just had to make sure I got close to you, keep you around, keep you alive, until it was time for the heavens to fall." The former police chief laced his fingers together and crossed his ankles in front of him. "Considering your penchant for diving into certain death at the drop of a hat, that wasn't always easy."

"Help me?" My voice betrayed my disbelief. "Motherfucker, are you that delusional?"

"Ever wonder why no one pulled you over when you high-tailed it from Virginia Beach to Hampton after the admiral died on the beach? Or why you were let go in the first place? A prime suspect just let to go home after such a high-profile killing? What about the little driving stunt your little slut pulled getting you to the church?" I let out a scream and tried lunging at Parkinson, only to be met by his fist in my forehead. Starbursts shot across my vision, and I squeezed my eyes shut to get my equilibrium back. "Me again. I could go on, but you get the idea."

"And you killed her!" I shouted, cords standing out of my neck from exertion.

"No, you did." Parkinson stood and walked to a high-backed chair that could easily double as a throne. He sat, his fingers steepled. "You had every chance to stay away from her, to end things, to make us have to wait another few years at least."

I spat on the dais, then caught the importance of his words. "You're not human, are you?"

"I was once. That was before."

"Before what?"

Parkinson let his hands fall to the arms of his chair and crossed his legs. "Oh no, Keeper. I've entertained myself enough for one night. This is the end of the line for you."

"Come on, you dick. One last question. What's it going to hurt?"

"Fine, but I won't answer about before. I want you to suffer eternity without that answer."

"I knew a cop had to be involved with the way the bodies at the sacrifice site were disappearing so cleanly. The only thing I can't figure is why. Was it because I disappeared?"

That earned me a look of admiration. "You catch on much too fast for your own good. For two years after the Fall, we didn't know how long the gods would stay down without sacrificing you. There was no way to know if the spell would last long enough for our purposes."

"So every week, you butchered someone in my place."

"It wasn't difficult to find candidates. In fact, for the first few months, there were volunteers galore. Granted, I told them it was simply losing the pinky finger off their left hand. A harmless lie for a great cause: keeping the gods where they belonged." Parkinson leaned to his right, stroking his chin in thought. "However, once it got out that we were being a bit dishonest, our search for candidates spread out. You see, we had to find those touched by the gods."

"Touched?"

"Oh, Statford, if you only knew." Eyes sparkling, Parkinson smiled as he leaned forward. "The sacrifices were those who could have been you."

"Potential Keepers?"

"Exactly. It was thought that, since you were gone, and no one could find you, we could use those who had that capacity as surrogates." He sneered at me. "Those deaths are also on your head."

"Suck your own asshole. I'm not the one who killed those people for some stupid ritual." My shoulders hunched under the hands of my captors.

"You know, the hell of it was, we didn't need to do it." Parkinson shrugged and sat back. "Apparently your little tantrum was enough to maroon the gods on this world, in this realm. There were a few exceptions, but they all had to come back here." He slapped his knee and laughed. "All that blood, all that death, for nothing."

"You are a sick fuck. I want you to know that, Hal, and I mean this from the bottom of my heart: I hope you enjoy dying by my hand."

Parkinson waved away the insult. "You have nothing else, Keeper. The knowledge you have is useless. The gods are here to stay, and you are not required to remain among the living."

"So what are you going to do, Hal?" I motioned to Mort and Tucker. "You're not man enough to kill me yourself? Gotta have underlings do it?" I shrugged. "That's cool. Morty and Tucker may be horsefuckers, but at least I know I'll be killed by actual people and not some hung-like-a-paramecium dickhole like you. Thanks. I truly appreciate it." I tried to struggle to my feet. "It's been real," I smiled.

The hands at my shoulders didn't let me get up, the one on the left exactly where I'd dislocated the joint before. I barely had time to look ahead when a wingtip came careening from in front of me, connecting solidly with my cheekbone. Something creaked in my face, and I hoped it wasn't my jaw. I fell over on my side with a grunt.

"You have no idea what I have lost, Keeper!" Parkinson kicked me in the stomach, my abused abdomen crying out in pain. "I had everything taken from me until I found the way to get it all back. It's not even for me! It's all for payback! All in revenge!"

I had no idea what he was talking about. It sounded like rambling gibberish someone says when they're stomping a mudhole in you. I bent over as best I could, trying to protect my stomach and ribs. I knew my head was a lost cause, covering my head with my hands wasn't going to happen right then.

Parkinson stayed away from my skull; apparently, he wanted to make sure I died conscious. Such a thoughtful guy. That didn't stop him from visiting hard kicks into every possible place below my neck. I've been worked over before, but this was an expert ass-beating. Considering that Parkinson was a dirty cop, I figured he knew how to hurt someone badly.

Finally after forty-seven kicks, each one designed for humiliation and damage, Parkinson stopped, his breathing heavy. He leaned over with his hands on his hips, trying to catch his breath. That sent the disgusting stench flowing over me, and I gagged. My reaction got a dry chuckle from the disgraced police chief.

"That was good, Keeper. That was very good. You bought yourself a few more minutes of life." The false good cheer was back, and I shuddered. To put it bluntly, Parkinson was nuts. "I won't let them kill you. That act is my right." To Mort, he said, "Get him on his knees."

"Yeah, Mort," I sneered. "Get me on my knees. You should know how that goes."

I was roughly set to kneel in front of Parkinson. My ribs creaked, my joints popped, and I gave a groan of pain as I settled into position. Mort stayed on my left, and Tucker remained on my right, both men holding me upright. I held my head up high, watching Parkinson return to his throne. He came back holding what looked like a revolver on steroids. I'd seen that kind of gun before: a .454 Casull, one of the largest wheelguns in the world. The bullets were so big, only five could fit in the cylinder. I had to hand it to Parkinson; when he wanted to kill you, he made sure he had the right tool for the job.

Of course, I couldn't resist. "Compensating, Hal?"

"One does not simply use one of your little guns for the task of pest removal. A real weapon is needed."

"And you have a tiny dick." The smirk on my face was designed to infuriate.

"Killing you is going to be a public service, Statford." Parkinson stood back, about three feet between the muzzle of his hand cannon and my forehead. "My only regret is not doing this years ago." He cocked the gun, the barrel looking like the entrance to a tunnel, and just as dark. "I always wanted to have a few choice words to send you to oblivion, but for the life of me I can't remember them."

"I have a few. 'I'm a psycho bitch with no dick.' How about 'I think about my men coating me in olive oil?'" I smiled widely. "I'm here to help."

"Not for much longer, murderer." He took careful aim and smiled. "Your time is done."

I took a deep breath and held it. My eyes were wide open, though; I would face the next few moments bravely. "Hit me with your best shot, bitch."

"Goodbye, Keeper." His finger went in the trigger guard, and I saw him sight down the barrel---

And *La Marseillaise* began to play. It was only the first few bars, but it was loud and coming from my inside coat pocket, accompanied by a buzzing.

Parkinson looked at me in disbelief, the gun lowering to point at the floor. He glanced at Tucker and Mort. "Really? You left him his phone?"

"That's how we were tracking him, sir." Tucker squeaked out his answer. "We didn't think anything of---"

The crash of the Casull from so close left my ears ringing and a strobe of muzzle flash on my eyes. Tucker's head exploded in gory fashion, bone and brain mixed with blood as the nearly-headless corpse fell to the floor next to me. There was almost nothing left of the top of Tucker's skull. Sluggish jets of blood came out of the hole, staining the wood.

"No, you didn't think." Parkinson sighed. Again the music went off. "Oh, Keeper, you just know how to ruin the moment. Why must your friend call you now?"

I looked up at Parkinson and smiled. It was one of the first real smiles I made in a very long time, and it felt so good. Yet again, the music played.

"What are you smiling about, you idiot?" Parkinson shouted, reaching into my coat and pulling out the phone. The case protected it well. "It isn't like I'm going to let you answer it."

Laughter burst from me, and there was no way I was going to hold it back. I felt Parkinson's and Mort's eyes on me, looking at me as if I had lost my mind. Mirth rolled out of me like a waterfall, and I could barely contain myself.

When I finally calmed down, I shook my head, my eyes boring into Harold Parkinson's. "You. Stupid. Shit. That call isn't for me.

"It's for you."

Chapter Thirteen

Okay, everyone, let's go find Sherman and Mr. Peabody and get the Wayback Machine up to eighty-eight miles per hour. It's time to see some serious shit.

The scene was my office, just a few days prior. Not too far back in time, so the memory was still crisp. This was before I woke up and made Renton lose a bet to Rika.

I was sitting in my office and scheming. Yes, I know only the bad guys are supposed to do that, huddle in their lairs and plot and scheme and plan for the eventual pain and agony of others, but I wasn't particularly feeling like a good guy. In fact, my thoughts were decidedly dark, as they had been since I fell out of the sky in front of my office. I was picturing the many terrible things I was going to do to the one who took my life away. Skinning, flaying, fileting… All that was merely foreplay for what I planned in my head.

I fed the rage, but I also wasn't stupid about it. There's the way it always goes in the movies. The lone hero, clad in the armor of righteousness, sallies forth all by himself toward the castle or lair or whatever of the villain, determined to right whatever wrong they could and do it without compromising their principles. There would be a fight, but there would never be any doubt as to the outcome.

After all, they are the hero, and who ever heard of the bad guy coming out on top? That was ludicrous!

Those same people are usually the ones who look at you blankly when you mention The Empire Strikes Back. Philistines.

Besides, this wasn't some movie or stupid pulp novel. This was real life. This was where real people could and did die, usually in astonishingly horrible ways. Friends and loved ones were lost to me because of choices I made or didn't make in time. People I cared about that were still alive carried the wounds, both visible and invisible. These were good people who didn't deserve any of what happened to them merely by their association with me. That such things were allowed was just proof that the gods were no more in charge of things than an ant in an ant farm.

And as it was real life, I was not under any delusion I was capable of fighting off the forces of evil by myself like some High Plains Drifter wannabe. Even though I was in much better shape than before, I was still a bit weak, mostly due to malnourishment and recovering from both mental and physical trauma. When you're an unwilling guest of Loki in the Norse Land of Mists, there aren't many places to get real food. Add to the fact I was still processing my grief that was delayed two years, and I wouldn't last three seconds in a straight fight.

So it was that dark and pleasantly cool night I came up with a plan, or The Plan, as I termed it in my head. It was a simple plan, with a lot of flexibility, and depended on a couple of very important things. The first, and absolutely most important part of The Plan was the loyalty of those I loved and trusted most. They were my support system, my backup, the foundation on which my life was possible. Rika, Renton, my mom, Luc, even Larry. Without them, I would have died a thousand times over, and death isn't always physical. I needed to trust they would come and help me when I needed it, no matter what. Most of all, I knew they believed in me.

The other part of the plan relied on my skill at being a complete and utter asshole. I needed to push everyone I loved away, no matter the cost, whether by word or deed. It was necessary for me to do so, because The Plan demanded I be flying solo.

That night, I wrote a series of letters. I chose paper and pen because I knew I was being watched, most likely electronically. That was about the time I started suspecting a cop or fed was in the mix; the number of times I got found by the Mayan cultists was far too often to be either mystical or coincidence. There were also the few times I went outside, mostly to the corner store for a sandwich or a six-pack of soda. My senses didn't lie; there were eyes all around me.

None in my office, thankfully; Renton was a fanatic about sweeping for listening devices, and the white-noise generator made all conversations in the office private.

There was also the fact I didn't have a new phone yet at that point, but that's neither here nor there.

"Larry," I said, both as a summons and an attention-getter. When the spirit appeared, I smiled. "Bad time?"

Dressed in a set of crimson silk pajamas, Larry smirked. "Even we need rest on occasion, Thomas. Your queries about Luvec's location have taken quite a toll. Of course the Baron still has him. You expected otherwise?"

I shook my head as I signed each letter with a flourish. "Nope. What about the other matter?"

"Something is happening in that warehouse. There is a body lying there now. Male, approximately forty. He is a member of the Order of Achilles." Larry cleared his throat. "He is missing his heart."

"Of course. I just wish I knew why."

"It likely has something to do with your disappearance."

"No bet there."

"You have finished?" Larry leaned over the desk to look. "Your handwriting is atrocious."

I rolled my eyes and snorted out laughter. That was the most handwriting I had done in literally years, and I massaged the cramp out of my hand. "Come on, it doesn't look that bad."

Larry raised an eyebrow. "It looks as if you are trying to send a series of illiterate ransom notes."

"Ha-ha, ha-ha, everyone's a godsdamned joker." I looked over each letter and re-read them carefully. "Seriously, man, what do you think?"

The letters generally went like this:

If you're reading this, Larry has appeared in front of you, and is telling you I need your help right the hell now. He isn't kidding; I'm probably about to get my damned fool self killed. Please understand, whatever I told you to push you away, I did not mean it. You are my family, and if you know me half as well as I think you do, you know what family means to me. It's all a ruse, as I'm under constant watch. I don't doubt my email is compromised, and my desk phone is tapped. This is the only way I can make sure no one else gets the message. Whatever I said or did to push you away, or hate me, or be disappointed in me, I'm sorry. You will always be my family.

When you're ready, call my phone. If I don't answer, come and get me. Good luck, and thank you.

I folded each sheet carefully into a triangle, what was called a football back in grade school. I wrote names on each one, my hand trembling only slightly when I finished. After that, the papers went into my pants pockets, since I couldn't be sure no one would break in and open my desk. Remember: it's not paranoia when they really are out to get you.

"What now, Thomas?" Larry looked a bit sullen. He didn't like lying to my friends and family any more than I did. His eyes did look a bit hollow, though that was likely due to all the searching he was doing at my bidding.

"Now comes the hard part, at least for me." I stood and faced Larry, who was leaning on my desk. "Until I say 'Go. Do my bidding,' you won't remember anything about those letters. What's more, you won't remember checking on the warehouse or Luvec. You'll actually want to avoid both like the plague."

"How does this help matters, Thomas?" Larry didn't like his memory messed with, and as someone who has had a chunk of their life erased, I understood his plight. "I would be able to serve you better if I know what is going on."

"This isn't about service, Larry." I rubbed my face with my hands, feeling the prickling of a couple days' beard growth. "I don't know if they can read your mind. If they could read mine, they'd have probably just killed me already. I need them to think I'm all alone again. It might allow me to get to the Big Bad and end this."

The spirit shook his head in amazement. "You want me to fear the warehouse?"

I nodded. "Not to the point of running away screaming, but you dread it. Anyone watching will see your reaction and take it as genuine. After all," I chuckled. "Spirits don't lie."

Larry sighed, a mean feat for a spirit. "Very well. I am ready."

"Forget until I tell your memory to return, my oldest friend," I intoned. It seemed ambiguously worded, but Larry knew me well enough to understand what I meant. He would keep the secret until I released the memory. "Now go rest. We have a long day tomorrow."

Larry's eyes closed and he faded away, like an old dream that vanishes just before the sun touches your eyelids. He looked pensive, but that was just the way he was. He would be a bit off until he was allowed to remember properly. Then again, so would I, since I was playing a game and no one else knew they were part of it, and no one knew the rules.

All that remained was getting to the right place at the right time, preferably with the son of a bitch responsible within my reach. I already had a going theory, but I needed confirmation. I wasn't about to go off and accuse someone of being the one who planned and executed the Fall, not unless I was completely sure.

That would need to wait, as I needed to sleep as well. The dreams were fading, though I still slept with the gun beneath my pillow. I had only drawn once, and it was on a shadow in the corner of my office. After that, I kept the door between my room and my office closed.

As I stripped down to my boxers and crawled between the covers, I wondered what it would be like to finally find the one who killed my wife as surely as that wizened old man's obsidian blade. In my mind, I kicked down a door and faced him down, gun drawn and ready to end his life the way he ended Susana's. Typical action movie crap, but it was always good for a chuckle. Doors were never that flimsy, and a hard kick would usually not do dick to a real door that someone locked against the outside. I modified it to shooting out the doorknob and kicking it in that way. That seemed more realistic.

I wondered what I would say. Would I be a smartass? Would I be completely serious? What would end up tumbling out of my mouth at the moment of truth? When the time came to tell this cruel bastard just what fate was about to befall him, would I be wrathful? Cold? Perhaps even forgiving? That was unlikely, but one thing I learned was the only thing set in stone is death. I could just become Mister Forgive-and-forget, completely blowing off the fact my wife, and by extension, my unborn child, were dead and I would never see them again. As I said, unlikely.

And finally, what would I do? Scream and threaten and just shoot him? Cut his limbs off? Perhaps give him a taste of his own medicine and see how well he did without his heart beating in his chest. Those thoughts kept me up until the wee hours, when I passed out.

What was I going to do; I was about to find out?

Chapter Fourteen

The last notes of the French national anthem echoed into the silence, and Parkinson's mouth was agape. He looked at me, a slowly dawning suspicion in his face. It took him only a second to get the superior look back on and raise his gun. My smile, on the other hand, never wavered.

"Let me guess: the French assassin?" Parkinson asked. He waved away any answer with his gun. "It doesn't matter. He and his ridiculous order won't get here in time to save you. By the time he gets here, your brains will be---"

The phone started buzzing again, this time playing the chorus of "Secret Agent Man" by Johnny Rivers. I was surprised at the volume my phone could put out; the guitars were crisp and clear, the vocals sounded like the man himself was singing. That was Renton, and I enjoyed the interruption. "You might have a problem, Hal," I mused as the phone stopped vibrating.

Parkinson gritted his teeth and roared, "It still doesn't matter! Two men can't stop this. This place will be your tomb."

Right on cue came the Police, singing about a message in a bottle. That did my heart good to hear, since it meant Mac had been notified. Knowing him like I did, he would have the place cordoned off and his SWAT teams keeping all of Parkinson's soldiers inside. "Wow. Did you learn how to suck this bad at being a bad guy in school, or does it come naturally?" I shrugged my shoulders again, my shoulders popping from the movement.

"Shut up!" His fist rocketed for my face, and I felt the impact. I felt the blow loosen my teeth a bit, but I sat up straighter, my grin never fading. "You will die tonight!"

Just then, Lady Miss Kier began to croon about grooves and hearts. I let out a breath I didn't know I was holding; that meant Rika was in the wings, ready to unload some unholy hell on anyone she could find. That brought out a laugh from me, which infuriated Parkinson to no end.

"You could start running now, Hal," I hissed, my jaw aching from the blow. Mort kept me upright, but he seemed less interested in sticking around and more interested in getting the hell out of there. When I looked up at Mort, his eyes were wide, and fear was etched on his face like a Day-Glo tattoo. "Seriously, Mort. You run now, you might live to talk about it."

"Enough!" Parkinson wrapped a hand around my throat and squeezed, bringing the gun to the center of my forehead. "They can't save---"

Tim McGraw broke in, telling the story of an Indian outlaw. I laughed and shook my head. Gods, even Harley came to join this ass-whipping. I owed that man more than I could say.

The former police chief and, at that moment, raving lunatic screamed in frustration, backing a few steps away from me. "This is impossible! You sent them away! We saw what you said to them, what you did to them. This can't be happening!" My phone dropped to the floor, bouncing on the wood before falling still and silent.

I said nothing. I just kept grinning at him, enjoying the way sweat was running down his face in runnels. Parkinson alternated hands with the Casull, wiping the empty hand on his pants while keeping the gun trained on me.

"You laughing fool!" Parkinson grabbed a handful of hair and yanked it back, shoving the gun under my chin. "We'll see just how your friends will like finding you after I paint the walls with your brains!"

My cloak of silence dropped. "Hal, I can tell you this with no hesitation. You've got one more chance to just put the barrel into your mouth. It'll be easier for me, and definitely easier on you, relatively speaking. There's only one other tone you might hear, and if we hear it, you're out of godsdamned time."

"You think you're going to scare me with tales of your friends coming?" I got a smack in the head from

Parkinson; his lieutenant Mort seemed to decide discretion was the better part of valor and started backing away before turning around and running away. He got maybe three steps before there was another boom, and Parkinson lowered his weapon, smoke coming from the barrel. Mort flew to the ground, a hole the size of a basketball newly arrived in his back.

"Good help is so hard to find these days, ain't it?" I quipped. "So what do you say, Hal? Give up? Let them end it quickly and relatively painless? Believe me, they will show you a mercy I never will."

At that moment, there came from the phone a deep and rolling tune. Horns played, and it was the fanfare all marches should have, with loud percussion and a rousing rhythm. It was the song that accompanied the dark lord of the Sith as he entered the scene. I began laughing, my body shaking from it. "Oh never mind, Hal. You just screwed every pooch on the east coast. You know who that is, and you are so fucked. I mean like sandpaper on the toilet paper roll fucked. There is no way this is going to go well for you."

Parkinson grabbed my throat again, this time pressing the barrel into my forehead. The gun was still warm from ending Mort's very brief career as Parkinson's lackey. There was madness in his eyes, the kind of insanity that spoke of terrible thoughts in the abyss between sleeping and awaking, that whatever were whispered in the dark was a good idea and should be shared with the rest of humanity. When he pushed me back onto the ground, I fell, the breath knocked out of me, but I remained smiling.

It was going to take more than that to even think of making me stop. With a low, raspy voice, I laughed. "Boy, did you find girlfriend-dick on this, Hal."

Parkinson pulled me closer, his rancid breath cloying in my face. "I will kill you, Keeper. I know you die protecting this world, and I know that you will die. It is all happening as it was told to me. I refuse to allow you to make me a disappointment!"

After taking another hit to the ribs, I figured he really wanted to get his frustrations out. "That's good, Hal. So glad we're getting through your anger." That remark earned me a knee to the chest. It was almost my jaw, but I moved out of the way. The gun, which was silver-plated, lashed out, loosening more teeth and my jaw in the process.

"You will die, Keeper! Die!" Another punch, this time with just his fist. "This is over now! You'll be dead before they get here!"

That statement nearly caught me unaware, and I leaned out of the way of his next hit, the gun passing harmlessly in front of my face. "What do you mean 'get here'? I didn't tell them to call me when they were on their way.

"I told them to call when they were ready."

The building rocked. I mean it actually swayed from an explosion from what felt like one of the lower floors. That was a toss up between Mom and Renton. Luc was a bit more subtle than high explosives, and I doubted Mac or Rika would go that far.

Well, not Mac, at least.

"I tried to tell you," I said, almost regretfully. Almost. "Your men are either dead or captured. Whatever you were planning just went down the shitter. You are well and truly boned, you stupid son of a bitch."

Parkinson's eyes were wide, not in amazement, but in fear. "So what? I give up, you take me in?" Wild laughter bubbled from his lips. "We both know that's not how this ends."

"No shit, Hal. I'm giving you the chance to make a choice." My voice was arctic. "Put that gun in your mouth or I'll be the one killing you."

Some of his composure came back. "You aren't much of a salesman."

Another explosion was followed by the rattle of automatic gun fire. That part was definitely Rika. "You don't have much of a selection."

"There is a third option." He put the gun against my head again. I was getting a bit tired of that maneuver. "I kill you, and even if they kill me, you'll be dead. A Pyrrhic victory at best."

"And you think I'm going to let you just kill me?" I shook my head . "You're high as a godsdamned kite."

"How will you stop me when you are completely defenseless?"

"Oh, you mean the handcuffs?"

The smile on Parkinson's face was insufferable.

My hands came from behind my back. The empty cuff dangled from my left wrist. "I picked them."

I clicked the cuff over his right wrist and pulled the gun out of line with my head. The trigger was pulled, the bullet destroying the huge circular picture window, and yanking both Parkinson's right arm and my left to the side from the recoil. I felt the tendons in my shoulder creak dangerously. It hadn't had the chance to heal properly, and there I was abusing it.

It was worth it.

The gun went flying and clattered to the floor. I sent a fist rocketing into Parkinson's no-longer-smug face, splintering his nose and sending blood spraying. The cuffs worked for me, letting me control his movements, yanking him around like a ragdoll and allowing me to rain devastation on his face and body.

Each punch was designed for maximum damage, hitting the jaw, the cheekbone, the solar plexus. Every hit connected, and I gave the bastard a good yank every now and again to keep him off balance. I was on my feet, dodging his ineffective counterattacks, pulling him into my fist, my elbow, my knees.

I put every bit of pain and rage and anger I had into each strike, relishing the crunch of bone, the grunts of pain, the flow of blood. "This is how it felt, you motherfucker!" I shouted in his face, pulling him closer to me. "This is how it feels to be yanked around like a godsdamned puppet, you sick fucking shit!" I pushed him away, then pulled him straight in so I could further destroy his face with a headbutt. "How do you like that shit?"

That was when he reached behind his back and pulled a knife the length of my arm. You have got to be kidding me.

I dodged the first swipe more by reflex and luck than by skill. I didn't expect him to have a knife. That spoke of either more planning than I thought someone would do, or sheer hubris on my part. The likely answer was somewhere in the middle, which wasn't all that comforting at the moment.

Parkinson stabbed at me, this time going after my caught arm. The tables had turned a bit faster than I liked, but I still had some advantage. His eyes were nearly swollen shut from the beating, and he was striking out blindly. I was still running out of ways to move and not get stuck, as the blade looked razor-sharp, and the point gleamed in the dim light.

"This is your end, Statford," Parkinson hissed, blood and flecks of teeth sputtering from his mouth. "This is the pain of thousands of years, the pain your kind has caused."

There was a weak swipe at me, which I dodged. "What the fuck are you babbling about?"

"For revenge, I will give anything. Will you?"

With that, Parkinson took the knife and, in one quick movement, shoved the knife into his trapped wrist. He screamed, more in fury than pain, and sawed off his own right hand. The knife must have been top of the line, because it took only three seconds for the tool to do the job. Blood spouted like a fountain out of the opened wrist, and his severed hand fell out of the cuff and onto the floor. The ragged flesh and muscle contrasted with the white bone and greyish tendons.

I fell back onto my ass and asked myself again: What kind of sick fucks was I dealing with?

"Now I'm free, Keeper!" Parkinson stumbled for the fireplace only a few strides away. With no hesitation, he shoved the stump of his right arm into the fire, and this time there was pain in that scream. If I wasn't horrified, I would have enjoyed that pain. As it was, I nearly retched from Parkinson's actions.

I scrambled to my feet as Parkinson's impromptu cauterization finished and he sprang at me, the knife flashing. His eyes seemed more open than before, and the blood wasn't flowing as freely as it had been a few moments before. That wasn't good. If I didn't end this soon, he was going to get all better and I was going to get all dead. Neither was a good option.

It was then Parkinson hesitated as his eyes focused behind me. Not wanting to take a chance, I didn't turn around, but I heard low chanting from there. I knew the voice, and I saw several dozen translucent forms appear in front of me. They seemed to be in a circle around me and Parkinson.

"Harley, that you?" I said, not taking my eyes off my enemy.

The deep baritone voice sounded from behind me. "Yeah, it is, you asshole. You gonna finish this?"

"What about these?"

"They want him for after."

I didn't question the statement. I just ran to Mort's corpse and grabbed the knife I could reach. His gun was under him, and as Parkinson chose that moment to attack, time was not on my side. His blade sank into Mort's back just as I slipped away.

"Now we're on even footing, Keeper," Parkinson sneered, yanking the blade out of the unmoving corpse. "Though I think I still have the advantage. You know what I'm willing to do to win. What will you do?"

"I have had enough of your shit!" I shouted, closing with Parkinson. His knife flashed out, barely missing my carotid artery. My move brought me in close, and my right hand came down from above. Parkinson raised his left arm to block the move and likely follow up with his own downward strike.

It would have worked, too, if the knife were in my right hand.

I couldn't say much for Mort, but he definitely kept his weapons in excellent condition. The point of the blade cut through the cloth and flesh and muscle of his stomach like smoke, and I felt the gush of blood on my hand. I lifted Parkinson up, using the knife as a handle, and ran him back into his throne. His blade fell uselessly to the floor as I twisted the blade, back and forth, knowing I was shredding his intestines with every move. His breath was hot, coming in putrid gasps in my face, but for the moment, I didn't care. I couldn't care. I enjoyed what I was doing, and knew it couldn't have ended any other way. I pulled back the knife and stabbed, again and again, relishing every single whimper and grunt and cry of pain. Body fluids sprayed on my hand, red and clear and a mixture of colors that belonged in no place in life, and I couldn't care. This was how it had to go.

Finally, I pulled away, leaving the knife in his gut. A horrid stench came from the wound, meaning I had done some major damage to his intestines and the contents were leaking into his bloodstream. Even if he could get to a hospital, the infection would probably kill him anyway. That wasn't even including the start of a massive flow from the wound, which meant I nicked his abdominal aorta. It probably wasn't more than a quarter-inch cut, but it was enough. I sure as hell wasn't getting him to a doctor.

And the son of a bitch was laughing.

"You're dying, Parkinson," I said. There was no more rage; I had left it in the destroyed abdomen of the man breathing his last in front of me. "It's over."

He shook his head. "Not yet." His stump was resting on the cavernous wound. I saw the muscles and organs moving through the hole in his stomach. "I know something you don't. I know who's in charge."

"It's not you." It was a statement, not a question. I bent over and picked up the Casull. It was heavy, too heavy for regular use, but it would do for what I had in mind.

"Save me, and I'll tell you." Parkinson's mouth worked around broken teeth and bleeding gums, and brackish blood coming up from his stomach. "There's still time."

"So you want me to save you? So you can tell me how to find someone?" I leveled the gun at him , the iron sights lined up with his forehead.

"You'll never find out who it is otherwise." The pleading note was there.

I felt the spirits Harley summoned around me, pressing against me. They were the ghosts of those Parkinson had killed for no reason, the useless sacrifices that were supposed to keep the gods on our plane, but weren't needed. They wanted their own pound of flesh, their own revenge on the one who orchestrated their deaths. Their hatred wasn't hot, but cold like an Appalachian winter.

"I'm a detective, Parkinson," I said. "Finding people is what I do."

Horror dawned on his face. "No! You can't!"

"I think it's time you met your adoring public." I pulled back the hammer on the Casull, the weapon heavy with judgement and purpose.

"No!" Parkinson held out his hand to stop me.

"Bang," I said. The gun echoed my sentiment.

I dropped the weapon to the floor and turned away. The spirits of the dead flowed by me in a chilling river, whispering their thanks to me for my actions. I said nothing in return. This wasn't for them. It was selfish vengeance and I was okay with that.

There were screams coming from behind me, barely audible, as if the maker of the scream was being pulled away inch by inch, and pulled apart bit by bit. My only thought on that? Good.

I walked to my phone and picked it up. Amazingly, the case had protected the device with no problems. I put it in my pocket and kept going.

I met Harley at the door. He was wearing body armor and a medicine bag around his neck. The stick he held was silent now, and he put it into his belt pouch for safekeeping. He had a sad smile on his face as he looked down at me. I put my hand out to him.

"Thanks, Harley." My face attempted a smile, which wasn't the greatest thing, but it was something.

He took my hand and squeezed it. "Ah, sometimes I like to work charity cases for assholes," he muttered. "It was your turn this week. Asshole."

We left the attic and took the elevator down to the lobby. It was covered in uniformed cops, SWAT members, and men and women in form-fitting black outfits. There were bodies on the floor everywhere, most of them not moving and a growing puddle of red beneath them. Those still moving were being led outside, where we went into the fresh cool Hampton air.

I took a deep breath of the sea, then another one. I felt a hand on my shoulder guide me towards a group of people standing around a black musclecar. The smile that lit my face could probably be seen for miles.

Renton stood stoic, a heavy machine-gun casually on his shoulder. He had his arm around Rika, who was cradling a military-style rifle. She sighed contentedly to herself and leaned her head onto Renton's chest. It wasn't a Harlequin romance, more like Guns and Ammo, but hey, who was I to judge?

Mac was in deep discussion with Mom, who stood in front of Luc. The assassin had his hood up, obscuring his features. He seemed somewhat uncomfortable in the light, but stood his ground. Mom seemed to be defending him, and letting Mac know, in no uncertain terms, that Luc and his people would be leaving unmolested, and any dead would be considered "assisted suicides." Mac shook his head and laughed and said the only thing he could in the face of that logic and the lady who presented it. "Yes, ma'am."

They saw me and waved, even Rika, who gave me an understanding smile. I knew I'd likely pay for what I said sometime, but I hoped she understood my reasons. I would accept the punishment, though, because she was a friend, my friend, and I would do anything for her. That's what friends do.

I looked up at the top of the Chamberlin, the broken window obvious to all who could see, and I felt my chest begin to loosen. My mind was clear, and my spirit felt lighter than it did. I sent a prayer up to Susana, hoping she was satisfied, and that she could and would rest easier.

"Then put your little hand in mine," I heard Sonny Bono sing from nearby. "There ain't no hill or mountain we can climb…"

My head swung around and locked onto one of the black-clad people walking by. I couldn't tell if it was a man or woman, but the music came from them. I was about to go after them when they pulled up their phone and answered it.

I laughed at myself. Whether that was a sign or just coincidence, it answered my question quite plainly. I let it go and walked to my friends and family, which for me was the same thing.

It was over, for now.

Epilogue

I slept like a rock that night.

The next day at my office, I met with everyone and apologized and begged forgiveness and groveled to the people I called friends after all I had said and done. That took about three hours, and it was not fun at all.

Surprisingly, Rika was the first to accept my apology. "I figured something was up. Even you aren't stupid enough to talk to me like that."

I laughed. "When did you figure it out?"

"After I plotted killing you in your sleep." She smiled sweetly.

I tell you, it's so wonderful to be loved.

"So Parkinson was behind it all?" Mac shook his head, nursing a diet soda. "It doesn't really make sense."

"It does if you look at the timeline." I ticked points off my fingers. "He showed up just before the godslayer. He was just in the right place at the right time for Raziel. He didn't do a damned thing about the Triads while they were in town, and even more, just let Susana get away with a confidential informant in her car. When did you know that glory-seeking bullshit artist let the identity of a CI go unknown?" I put my hands down on my desk, the solid wood a comfort. "He knew I was in the car. He also made sure Susana and I could only go to New Orleans when we did.

"But he wasn't behind it all." My words rang out in the silence, everyone present absorbing the statement. "Whoever was backing him is still out there, and we have to be ready."

"Are we going hunting for this puppetmaster?" Luc's mouth quirked in anticipation. I had a feeling he possessed his own reasons for wanting to get the party started.

"No, not yet. We did a lot of damage to his network, kicked over the anthills, so to speak." I smiled. "If anything, we'll be the hunted ones, but not for a while. They need to lick their wounds."

"Good," Renton said. "That means we can give you this." Renton held out a car key.

I think I actually blushed. "Come on, man. I appreciate the offer, but I don't think that musclecar is really my speed."

Renton laughed at that, then saw my face. "Oh, wait, you were serious?" He then laughed harder. "Go outside."

I did so, and came to a screeching halt. My mouth fell open and I think I made some kind of noise when I saw the jet-black Jeep in the parking lot. It gleamed under the sunlight of a beautiful southeastern Virginia sky, the sun unimpeded by any clouds. I traced the hood with my hand, sheer admiration in the gesture. The wheels were off-road types, and I knew the model was a four-wheel-drive, with enough oomph in her to get me where I needed to go in a hurry. There was even a winch on the front, which was a very nice touch.

"She isn't the Black Beauty," Renton said, putting the key in my hand, "but she will get you around. Besides, my job is agent, not chauffeur." The light tone robbed the words of any bite.

And before anyone asks, yes, I hugged him. Shut up.

An hour later, everyone except Mom had left. She stuck around to help me clean up the victory party. I tried to tell her she didn't have to, but I might as well have been talking to a wall. We were silent as we picked up the empty bottles and cans, the pizza boxes, the napkins. I was mostly in my own thoughts.

Was it over, even if only for a little while? When it began again, who was behind all of it, and most importantly, why? Would I have time to prepare?

Most importantly, who else was I going to lose?

I pushed away those ideas as I shoved a six-pack of beer bottles in a garbage bag. That filled it and I closed it up.

What would happen, would happen in the course of time. I couldn't stop it, but I would be ready.

Or I would, after I did one more thing.

"Well, that's everything, Tommy." Mom sounded bright and chipper, even though I knew she had slept maybe four hours in the last forty-eight. She was in jeans, boots, and a Virginia Tech jacket. "I'll be going now. I know you need your rest. You had a long night."

As she turned to leave, I said, "Hey, Ma? Got a minute?"

The tone in my voice turned her around instantly. "What's wrong?"

I sat on the sofa and put my head in my hands. The light from outside was in my face, the windowed door letting the sun through. My hair was still growing back, and the stubble was a bit longer. "I need to talk."

Mom took a seat across from me, pulling a chair from in front of my desk. Her smile was sweet and genuine as she took my hands. "You can talk to me. You know that."

I took a deep breath and began. "After Susana died, I didn't know where I was, or who I was. I woke up somewhere, and some doctor had just done some electroshock on me." It was about then the tears started to fall.

As the story of my time in Niflheim poured out of me, I saw the new placard was painted on my window. Even backwards, I could read it without a problem.

Thomas Statford. Private Investigator. Keeper of the Conclave.

Yeah, I liked the sound of that.

Thank you again for following me on this ride, but it's not over yet. This is just the end of the beginning. Tom Statford will return, and you ain't seen nothing yet.

Afterword

So… here we are.

I don't mind tell you all I didn't think I'd make it this far. Hell, I didn't even think I'd get past the first book. I thought the Statford Chronicles would be just a Chronicle, and the manuscript would remain a file that would go from one hard drive to another, kind of like a drawer novel of the electronic age. I would take it out, read it to myself, marvel at it, and wonder why I just didn't go for it and try to get it published. I'd see my friends talking about people they know putting out amazing book after book and just writing. I thought it would be too difficult, and that I wasn't that good a writer anyway, and who would want to read about a guy who talks to gods and saves the world, or at least his little corner of it?

And yet… here we are.

I can't say I'm a great writer; I can say I've improved a hell of a lot. I can also say I'm never more alive than when I'm stressing myself thinking of the next idea, the next scene, the next paragraph, the next word. Chasing thoughts, beating them into ingots of usable ore, then shaping them in the crucible of the keyboard, scraping away the extra garbage and being left with what the man I call a mentor and a friend would call "literary gold."

There is so much I could say about this book. I could tell you that it hurt to write it, that I felt I wasn't quite ready to write it. Not mentally, at least. I could have gone through the motions, put in a few pithy Statfordisms, made everyone and everything live happily ever after. I could have just waved a magic wand and all would be well.

That's not how life is, though. Life is not the happy endings, the hero riding off into the sunset, the neat and tidy story where every question is answered with no loose ends. Life is the journey to those sunsets, the pain to get there, the struggle to make it one more day... hell, one more step, just to be closer to making it. It's almost never fun and games, and it leaves scars, some visible, some not.

Regardless, it's how you accept those challenges and problems, and how you knock the living shit out of them to make it, because you'll be damned if you're going to let it stand in your way. That isn't your way, and it sure as hell isn't my way.

So... here we are, where the end of the beginning starts. After I got the whole story mapped out (yes, the entire story is already in my head), I knew I'd have to do it right. Enter the idea in my noggin about having the first few books setting up the world and the characters *before* the story really starts! Everyone knows the trope of the grizzled and cynical detective, but you don't know why, except through flashbacks or veiled references. The Chronicles, at least the first seven books, set up the why, and also the where. It really struck a chord in me, and I have to say: this is how prequels should be done, which is before anything else. Make a note, Hollywood.

By now, I know the characters. I know the world, even though it's very much changed from the almost-normal world we know after book five. I know how it all works, and I think everyone else does, as well. There are still a few surprises left, though, if this book is any indication. I've found my characters have no problem making me wonder just what the hell they're going to do next.

There was one big surprise, though, at least for me personally. When I first went to Balticon, the fantasy/sci-fi writer's convention in (where else?) Baltimore, Maryland, I felt like the biggest fraud. I mean, there I was with a measly three or four books under my belt while some really big people with several series, a smattering of awards, and visual recognition by actual fans were walking around. It's called Imposter Syndrome, and I had it in spades. As long as you're a writer, you'll get hit by it at the worst times.

This last Balticon, though, I had a few amazing things happen. I was interviewed by Gus Grappin and Erin Kazmark of the Melting Potcast, which you should totally fill your ears with, but I also got a fan letter.

I mean it. An actual letter. On paper and everything.

A feather could have knocked me over. That was the most touching thing I've gotten as an author. Whenever I start to doubt I know what the hell I'm doing at a keyboard, I pull out that letter and read it. I think of how someone actually liked my work enough to send me a fan letter, and it gets me through those dark times.

So now, at this point in the Chronicles and my writing career, I can say that, in all likelihood, I will get hit by that Imposter Syndrome. I know other writers and artists get it. However, I know that I can beat it. I know that I can write. I've written and published seven books. I had a New York Times best-selling author say I was good. I have several other ideas brewing in my head, and they are actually fantastic.

But that letter… That letter is what helps me realize that I'm not just talking to the crowd.

That letter tells me someone is listening. Thank you, Anthony.

Okay, so enough navel-gazing. Thank you all for reading this, and yes, the Statford Chronicles are not done yet. We've a good while to go. Wait til next year. It's going to be completely epic, and just the start of a new arc in not just Tom's life, but my own.

See you all then.

John G Walker

November 9, 2015